Drilled: A Blue Collar Bad Boys Book

Blue Collar Bad Boys, Volume 3

Brill Harper

Published by Brill Harper, 2017.

DRILLED: A BLUE COLLAR BAD BOYS BOOK

First edition. July 7, 2017.

Copyright © 2017 Brill Harper.

ISBN: 979-8223109587

Written by Brill Harper.

About This Book

Graden

Four years ago, my buddy's dying words to me were to watch out for his little sister.

I did what he asked from afar, and when she graduated and got a job teaching kindergarten, I asked her to "housesit" for me since I'm hardly ever home when I'm working on the oil rig.

But now I'm injured and have to recuperate at home, and my extra-curvy housesitter is anything but safe from me.

She's the homebody type. She'll make some man an excellent wife someday, be a good mother. She likes taking care of people. It would be wrong AF to take her the way I want to, but it would feel so right.

When she comes to me for advice about how to get a boyfriend and how to keep him, I'm done playing her silent guardian.

I'll teach her everything she needs to know about pleasing a man—me.

She says all she's ever really wanted to do was be a mama. And now I can't stop thinking of putting my baby in her belly.

AUTHOR'S CONFESSION: This story is trope soup and I loved every minute of writing it. Don't believe me? Older man/ younger woman. First time. Roommates. Older brother's best friend. BBW heroine. Alpha real man hero. Guardian/Ward. Breeding romance. Insta-lust. Heck, if I'd have given one of them amnesia, we'd have a serious drinking game!

Chapter One

GRADEN

My roommate is giving me a hard-on.

She's breezing in and out of the room now because she's getting ready to go out on a date. It's just as well. She smells too damn good, and one of these times she passes by me on the couch, I'm liable to reach out and pull her down to me. Mold my hand around those curves. Kiss those heart-shaped lips that haunt my dreams all night long and tempt my control in the daylight hours.

She doesn't know what she's doing to me. How she's awakened the...I guess you'd call it...beast...inside me. Hell, if she knew about the things I want to do to her, she'd pack a bag and run.

But that's just it. Where would she go?

I've spent the last four years taking care of her from afar, but she doesn't know it. She doesn't know the renewable, annual scholarship that paid her tuition, room, and board all through college was funded by me. She doesn't know the car she "won" is a gift from me, either.

And the condo? It's mine, too. That she knows. She was supposed to be housesitting for me while I was out on the oil rig. But until I'm done with physical therapy and my foot injury is healed enough to go back to work, my ass is planted on this couch during the day and the guest room at night.

Yeah, I sleep in the guest room of my own house.

I only bought this condo so Rebecca would have a safe place to stay. I had to buy furniture to make it look even a little lived in. I used to just have a small shitty apartment and storage unit to store what little stuff I owned. I spend most of my life on the oil rig where I work. When I have time off, I usually travel on my Harley or park my ass on a Mexican beach. Away from people. Away from women I could hurt.

I don't like hurting women.

So sure, I told her to take the master suite when I asked her to move in. I made sure it had a luxury bathroom because chicks dig that shit, and I wanted her to live here a long time so I could easily keep an eye on her.

I'm not a stalker or anything.

I'm just a man of my word. I made a promise to her brother.

My best friend, Rebecca's older brother Cameron, was in a bad car wreck four years ago. There was nothing I wouldn't do for my buddy, he was more like my brother than a friend, so when he made me promise to look out for his baby sister, I vowed to him I would.

And then he died.

This is not what he meant when he asked me to take care of her. The way I imagine defiling her over and over again. She's too sweet for a guy like me. Too pure.

She was raised to be a good girl. From a good family. Cam and Rebecca's parents are respectable people, but not rich people. Cam had been helping them with bills and had been planning on helping with college for his baby sister. His dying left them in a bad place, emotionally and financially. I'm not rich or anything, but I make damn good money, and I don't spend much of it. So, I played like Santa's fucking elf and took care of shit.

But Cam's baby sister isn't a baby anymore. Something I wasn't prepared for when I moved back into the condo for the summer.

She's fucking stacked. She's round everywhere, man. Her body has got my hands itching. I want to map every hill and valley of her lush figure with my tongue. She's not slender, like the women I usually get hot for. She's plumper. Womanly. Like those fertility statues in museums. It makes me want to grab her everywhere.

I want her as mine.

She's too young. Too innocent. And she wants the kind of life that includes a picket fence and family portraits on Instagram. I'm not that guy. I'm the guy who could fuck her, and fuck her well. But that's it.

I'd wreck her, though. I'm too brutal. Too rough. Too big. Everywhere.

"Graden? How's your foot?" She's standing in front of me adjusting her purse on her shoulder. Because she's ready to go. On her date.

I want to punch a fucking wall, but I've got no right.

"It's fine." My foot hardly ever bothers me, but the doctors say my threshold for pain is high, too high, so I need to be even more careful. I don't like feeling like a wuss and doing nothing when I should be working, but if I reinjure it because I don't feel the pain, I could end up permanently unable to go back to my job.

"Did you take your pill?" She's holding my prescription, rattling the pills in the bottle. I hate those things.

"I don't need one."

"Graden, you know what the doctor said."

I give her what I hope is a reassuring smile. "I'm not in any pain. Now go. Text me when you get there so I know you're safe."

"Okay, Daddy." She sticks her tongue out at me.

Fuck me. I know she means it in a funny, sarcastic way. But all I can think of is her calling me "Daddy" when I'm pumping my cock into her. And that tongue she stuck out, the dreams I've been having about that tongue...

I need to get back to work on the rig. There is no way I can survive the summer in close quarters with her and keep our relationship platonic. She thinks of me like some kind of foster big brother. I'm supposed to think of her like a sweet, baby sister.

But I don't. I used to. But I don't anymore. Not since I saw her for the first time in the flesh last month. Back when Cam was alive, I saw his pictures of her and they never did anything for me. She was cute then. Awkward. A kid. After he died, I saw her once at the funeral. I kept in contact with her parents, and she and I texted sometimes or emailed. But I hadn't seen her since. I didn't know.

She's a woman now. A beautiful one. But a sweet one. Somehow naïve despite the world we live in. Cam would expect me to honor that. Take care of that innocence.

Not fuck it right out of her. Like I want to.

And so, instead of hooking my arm around her waist and bringing all that softness into my lap, I send her off on a date with someone else. I don't get to be territorial.

But I swear to God I want to kill this Trent or whatever the fuck his name is that's taking her to a ballgame. I'm pretty sure she doesn't even like baseball. I doubt he cares.

"Dinner is in the fridge. You just need to nuke it to warm it up." She does that. Every night now.

"You don't have to cook for me. I'm not an invalid. I can cook my own food." My words come out short and grumpy. Which is how I feel, but she doesn't deserve that.

"I know I don't have to. I like taking care of you. Besides, it's the least I can do when you let me live here rent free."

"You're doing me a favor. I don't like leaving this place empty." I shake my head. "Sorry I snapped at you. You know I love your cooking, right?" Because I do. It's like...this is going to sound stupid...but it's like I can feel how much she cares in each bite.

She leans down and kisses the top of my head. Her tits are in my face, and it takes everything I have not to grab them and suck on them through that damn T-shirt.

As soon as she goes, I'm going to have to rub one out because my balls are fucking full.

She gets to the door when her phone dings, and she looks down at the message. Her face falls. Her lips press into a tight line, and her hand starts to shake. I'm across the room before I realize I've gotten up. "What's wrong?"

She shakes her head. "Nothing."

Fuck that shit. I take her phone, hold her wrist when she tries to get it back. I read the message.

Decided I don't want you to get the wrong idea, babe. Just want to be friends. Best we skip game. Taking my brother instead.

That little fuck.

"May I have my phone, please?" Her voice is strained.

"He's a punk."

"Whatever." She takes her phone back. "I'm just going to go lay down for a while. I have a headache."

I haven't let go of her wrist. "Don't do that. Don't let the punk who wasn't good enough for you make you feel bad. He's an asshole."

"You don't even know him."

"Any guy that cancels at the last minute by text is an asshole. I promise. You deserve better."

Shit. She's starting to tear up. I don't know how to handle her tears. I can barely handle her smiles. They make me try to think of shit to keep her happy. But tears, man, I will rip the arms off the bastard if it stops her tears. I'll do whatever the fuck she needs to never see them fall.

"I'm not really sure I deserve better anymore. It's starting to feel like I don't deserve anyone at all." She frowns at me while looking at my foot and then over to the couch. "You left your cane over there."

She brings it to me, and I grab her around the middle and make her sit on the couch with me. "Tell me what's going on."

Rebecca covers her face with her hands. "I don't want to."

"Becks," I growl. I can't fix it if I don't know. Did she really like that guy? Should I go drag his ass back here?

"I need some kind of intervention. I'm so stupid."

"Now you're pissing me off. There's nothing about you that is stupid. What's going on?"

"There *is* something wrong with me, and I really don't think you're the person I can talk to about it."

That kind of hurts, and I don't know why.

"You can tell me anything."

"Not this."

I'm holding in a growl. Actually, it's more like a primal howl. She's holding back from me. Hiding something from me. It should be her own damn business; she owes me nothing at all. But tell that to the caveman inside who thinks she belongs to us.

"You can tell me anything. I'll always help you. You know that."

"I don't think you want to help me with this. Nobody, it seems, wants to help me with this."

I'm trying to be patient. Really, I am. "Have I ever let you down?"

She looks at me, her eyes shining. "No. You're the best man I know, Graden."

"Well, that's pushing it." I swipe my thumb across her cheek, wiping away the wetness before I give in to the urge to taste her tears. "Just tell me what the problem is. I'll make it better. You know I will. I can fix damn near anything."

"The problem is…oh God, I can't believe I'm telling you this. The problem is that I'm a virgin."

Chapter Two

REBECCA

I want to reach out and pull the words back into my mouth. But they are out there now, and Graden looks like I just slapped him across the face.

"You're a virgin?"

Like, is this the worst thing in the world or something? I mean, it's a little annoying to me, but why is this some big issue for him? "Never mind. It's not a big deal."

"Were you going to give it to him?"

Now I feel like the one who got slapped. *It*? Crass much? "Maybe I was. It doesn't matter now, does it? Trent didn't want it. *Nobody* wants it." And I am making this hole so much deeper than it needs to be. But hey...I can crawl into it and hide now.

"Why?"

"Why what?"

He leans back against the cushion. "Why are you still a virgin? Why were you going to give it to him? Why nobody else? I don't know. I'm trying to figure out what's going on."

I want to tell him it's none of his business. But I guess I made it his business when I told him. "In high school, I wasn't ready when the rest of my friends were. In college, I don't know...I was still sad about my brother, and then I was just too busy to worry much about guys. And now it sort of feels like this anchor. Like something I want to get rid of. But then again, I've waited this long, so it feels like I should at least be serious about someone. At the very least, third date material. Except, I can't seem to get a second date. Which means no third date." I cover my face again. This is too much. Graden does not need to know this.

He pulls my hands back down. He's shifted so he's hovering a little so he can keep my wrists at my side. "Why?"

"That's what I'd like to know. At first I thought it was my body." I look down at my obvious curves. My many obvious curves.

"There is nothing wrong with your body."

I shrug. "I know I'm not skinny. And I get asked out on first dates, so I don't know, some guys like their women plump, I guess. But everything just fizzles out on the dates. Sometimes I know it's not going anywhere, so I don't expect a call, or I ask them not to call. But lately, I've been willing to at least try date number two...but it never surfaces. Maybe they can smell my desperation." I look into his dark eyes. They are so intense. So focused on me. I have to swallow hard. My throat feels tight. "Do I smell desperate to you?"

I tilt my head to look at him. His face is close. I can feel the heat of his skin. His breath on me. The world pauses for a second until he blinks like he's waking up. "You smell like cookies to me."

I inhale sharply. His words kiss something inside me, and my belly tightens.

"Cookies?"

"Yeah. You smell good, babe."

I have to laugh a little. He doesn't pay compliments like most people. But you never have to wonder if he means what he says. There's nothing artificial in his words. Ever. If he says I smell like cookies, that means he likes how I smell because I've seen how much he likes cookies.

"I don't know what I'd do without you, Graden." Sometimes I wonder what I'd do *with* him, if given the chance. Graden is like every dream, every fantasy, I've ever had rolled into one extra-large, extra-handsome package. Nothing about him is soft or sweet at first glance. He's big, beastly really. Every muscle comes from hard work. But the sweetness is there, under the rough exterior.

He thinks of me like a little sister, though. And I just worship him from afar. If I can't get a guy like Trent, there's no way I could get a guy like Graden. I don't know the kind of women he dates, but I can guess. Not chubby girls who teach kindergarten who've never seen a penis up close that wasn't on a porn site.

So, yeah, getting distracted now.

"Well, there are worse things to smell like than cookies," I say. "But then I still don't know what's wrong with me. All I've ever really wanted was a family of my own, and maybe that's the problem. Even though I don't wear a sign that says, "I want to get married and have your babies," that's what they sense. But I don't want to just jump into a committed relationship any more than they do. I just want to see where things could go." I pat his knee. "I really am going to go lay down for a while. I think I need comfy clothes and Mr. Darcy."

"Who is Mr. Darcy?"

I roll my eyes. "*Pride and Prejudice.*" He looks at me blankly. "Jane Austen. None of that rings a bell?"

He shakes his head. "Nope." He stops me from getting up. Just thrusts one well-muscled arm out. "There is nothing wrong with you."

"I just need to be alone. I'll be fine." Is it wrong that something about his forceful hold on me makes me press my legs together? It's...hot. Maybe my alone time will include some...me time.

"Bring the movie out here. We'll watch it together." I start laughing. "What?" he asks. He looks so serious. And seriously confused.

"I don't think it's your kind of flick."

"Bring it out."

"You'll hate it."

"If you like it, I'll like it."

"No, you won't. But okay. I'm feeling just mean enough to make you sit through it."

Chapter Three

GRADEN

I fucking hate it.

Everything about it. It's boring. I can't understand what they're saying. Nobody bangs anybody and there are no car chases.

But Rebecca is curled up on me asleep, and I'm not moving.

Maybe ever.

Everything about her is soft and pleasing to me. I want to explore every curve with my hands and my mouth. See if she tastes as sugary as she smells.

I got it bad man.

And she's cherry.

Shit.

I don't know what to do with that information. I know what I want to do with it. She thinks it's an anchor, but to me it's a beacon. A homing signal. I want to be her first...and her last. That's the scary part.

She deserves a guy who'll marry the shit out of her and keep her pregnant and happy. Take care of her. Be her partner. Me? I don't know how to do that. There's a reason I work on a fucking oil rig in the middle of the goddamned ocean, man. I never wanted hearth and home and whatever goes along with it. I like knowing my life can fit in a rucksack if I need it to. I don't want a wife or kids or a house.

But I wish I did. I wish I could step up into that life and take my place next to Rebecca. Haul her ass to the altar. Keep her in bed until I plant enough of my seed in her to make her a mama.

My cock sure as hell likes the idea. But that monster needs to take a fucking time out.

She stirs a little in her sleep. She's got on plaid drawstring pajamas and a T-shirt. No bra. Fuck. I need to stop looking at her tits. But they're so pretty. Soft, round melons that make me ache. I can see the faint outline of her nipples, and that's crossing the line, so I tear my gaze away and it lands on a strip of skin exposed between her shirt and pants. It looks so soft. Lickable.

Rebecca snuggles deeper into me and I feel the tree trunk in my pants grow even harder. This isn't right. I shouldn't want her so much. She's not trying to be sexy—she's just being herself. Just trusting me. I'm the biggest asshole.

"Why are you scowling?" Her voice startles me as she sits up, stretching her neck. "Your foot hurting?"

"No, sorry. Just deep in thought."

She yawns and stretches, her shirt riding up a little more. I'm doomed. "Sorry I fell asleep."

"Nothing to be sorry for."

She cocks her head at me, her gaze inquisitive. "Are you mad at me?"

"No."

"Really? Because your jaw is rigid, and there's a little tic thing happening in your mandible and you practically growled at me when you said no."

I take a deep breath. "I'm pissed at the asshole who made you feel bad. That's all."

She pulls her legs crisscrossed, getting comfortable, and I feel this weird feeling of pride that she's settling in to talk to me. Like we're friends. Like this could be what we did every night if we always lived together. Her sitting cross-legged on the couch looking at me like I had all the answers.

A guy could get used to it.

Don't.

"You should help me," she says.

"Help you what?"

"Figure out what I'm doing wrong. With men. Like a class...Real Man Seduction 101. You could teach me how to entice a guy like you."

Holy fuckballs.

"What are you talking about?"

"Well, obviously, I'm not doing something right. I need a guy's perspective. Someone who will be honest with me and steer me the right direction. I want to know how to get and keep the interest of a guy like you."

"A guy like me?"

She nods. "Yeah, a guy like you." She looks at me and pales. "You have total resting bitch face or you're pissed. Why is this making you mad?"

I try to relax my face, but she's mistaken about the anger. I'm not mad. I'm feeling about ninety percent caveman right now. I don't want to scare her or make her uncomfortable, but I want to pull her under me and take her. Hard. It's bad enough she just asked me to help her, but help her get with another guy? Every cell in my body is rebelling like it's wrong. Like she belongs to me and me alone. And like I should show her with my cock who she belongs to.

I take a deep breath and will my muscles to loosen the fuck up. "What is a guy like me?"

"Are you fishing for compliments, roomie?" She tosses a pillow at me. "Well, aside from being sexy, you're confident. In charge. You know how to take care of things. You're a real man. You're honest, straightforward. You don't ask women out and then text them when you change your mind. When I'm with you, I feel safe, like nothing could hurt me. Like you'll take care of me. That's how I want to feel."

That's how she wants to feel with another guy.

But shit, she thinks I'm sexy.

"I think you deserve a guy better than me, sweetheart. I wasn't raised right. No role models. A series of strange men who would pretend to be my buddy for the three weeks or so they could handle being with my mom and then they were gone. She was...unstable. And some of those guys...let's just say the sooner they left the better. She wasn't good at picking winners. It wasn't until your brother came along that I even had a real friend."

Her face goes all soft. "I didn't know that. I guess we never talked about family before."

"Not much to say." I don't want her pity, that's for sure. But I do like all her attention focused on me like this. She has a way of making me feel like a better person than I am.

"My folks are great. A little...old-fashioned and always more broke than not. But Cam and I had good examples. I want a relationship like theirs." She sighs. "But I can't seem to find the right guy."

"You're setting your bar too low. That's your problem with men. It's not you; it's them. You're dating the wrong ones, is all."

She shakes her head. I want, God do I want, to show her how amazing I think she is. I don't have the kind of words she needs. The ones she deserves. Someone who has a better education than I do is who she should be looking at. Someone who has better manners and can guide her through society better. A guy who'll give her all the babies she wants. Someone who knows how to love a woman.

And whoever that asshole is, I hate him for being what she needs. What she's really looking for. I hate him for not being me.

"I'm dating the guys who ask me out. If they are the wrong ones, then I need help finding the right ones to ask. So, how does a girl like me get a guy like you interested?"

I need off this couch. Out of this room.

"You just need to be yourself, baby. That's all. You don't need to do a damned thing to be desirable. You already are."

She's turtling up because she doesn't believe me. I can see her withdrawing. Her body curls into itself as she pulls her knees up and hugs them. "I get it. I shouldn't have asked for your help."

"Becks, look at me."

She does and, fuck, I'm lost. Those sweet baby-blues are watery. I can't let her cry. Not when all she needs is for me to help her find her confidence.

"Sweetheart, you are beautiful. You told me you think I'm honest, so believe me when I tell you that. I won't ever lie to you. You're safe with me. And if you need something from me, you will get it. Always. Whatever you want."

"Whatever I want?" She gets this mischievous grin I haven't seen before. "Then what I want is for you to help me seduce someone just like you. Tomorrow, we're going to the mall and you're going to help make me over."

"The mall?" I fucking hate the mall.

"You said anything. Besides, you're supposed to get a little exercise for that foot every day. We'll get some walking in, and then you can prop it up the rest of the day."

"What do you want at the mall?"

"An outfit or two that doesn't make me look like a kindergarten teacher would be nice."

"You are a kindergarten teacher." Why doesn't she want to look like one? I like the soft clothes she wears. The way she always looks ready for a hug. Like she isn't afraid of getting mussed up.

"I want to entice a man into bed, Graden. I need him to look at me like I'm a sex-toy made for pleasure, not a frumpy teacher."

Fuck. Me.

Chapter Four

REBECCA

As we walk through the mall, I'm sort of pretending that Graden is my boyfriend. Just imagining what it would be like to have him as mine. I know it's a fantasy, but I indulge anyway, noting how women eye-fuck him as we go by.

He doesn't seem to notice them. Which makes me wonder what it takes to get him to pay attention. What does he find attractive?

"Underwear," he says, stopping in front of a lingerie store.

"What?" I ask. Had I asked him what he found attractive out loud? God, I need to be careful what I think if I can't keep my thoughts in my head where they belong. He would be so embarrassed if he knew how often I pretended he was mine. How when I made him dinner, I'd fantasize about what it would be like to be married to him. How I think about what it would be like if he didn't go to the guest room at night but instead carried me into the master suite like it was our room. Our bed.

"That's where you should start."

I have to rewind to remember what we were talking about before my mind drifted to my mental marriage with the man least likely to even see me as a woman, much less a woman he wanted to carry to bed.

"Start what?" I ask.

He looks at me like I am crazy. "You wanted a makeover. You should start with underwear."

"What's wrong with my underwear?" Has he even seen my underwear?

Is he blushing? "Nothing. I mean, I haven't seen your underwear, but I'm sure there is nothing wrong with it. But if seduction is on your mind, then start here."

I sigh. This store is definitely not the kind that caters to girls with my figure. "Men can't see what underwear I'm wearing before they ask me out. I need to get them to notice me first. That's my first mission."

I start to walk again, but he grabs my hand and keeps me there. "The underwear isn't for them; it's for you," he says. "If you know you are wearing sexy panties underneath your clothes, any clothes, you'll feel sexier. And that is what attracts men. Your sweet little secrets are for you to know, and him to be dying to find out."

"Oh," I say, dumbly. He's still holding my hand, and I want him to never let it go. "Is that real? Or did you make it up?"

Because the words coming out of his mouth don't sound anything like the Graden I've come to know over the last few years. At all.

"Honestly, I read it in the *Cosmopolitan* at the doctor's office yesterday. The issue was from 2013, but I think it's still valid."

I can't stop the giggle that bubbles out.

"What?" he asks, pretending to be defensive. "Can't a guy read a magazine?"

We both start laughing, and then we stop and have this awkward moment where we have dopey smiles on our faces, but nothing is funny anymore. And I like seeing this side of him. Awkwardly Smiling Graden is endearing. And if I'm being honest, makes him all that much hotter.

I guess it's time to admit to myself that I don't want a guy "like" Graden, I want Graden. I know he sees me as a little sister. I'm not his type at all, which I guess is why we're here. So I can figure out what his type even is. Not that I could change his mind about me. But maybe there is a Gradenesque model out there somewhere. And he's just waiting for me to stumble into the lonely bar he's waiting in. Maybe *Cosmo* is right, and I need the underwear to trick myself into thinking I'm sexy.

Nevertheless, this store is intimidating.

"I'm not sure, Graden."

"Come on." He pulls me inside.

A too-beautiful-to-be-a-shopgirl woman greets us, and I immediately want to slink out. Her name tag says *Leslie,* and when she asks how she can help me, my tongue ties. I don't know. I don't want to be here, so helping me would include showing me the quickest way out of the store.

She's eyeing Graden like a snack, but pauses on our still linked hands. I expect her to give me a catty reply or look, but instead, she gives me a secret wink.

"My girlfriend wants to buy something that will knock my socks off," he tells her when I still haven't answered. I inhale sharply at the word "girlfriend" and wonder how it would feel if he wasn't pretending. "But all I know about lingerie is what I think will look good on my floor."

Oh, God. The mental pictures I'm having are indecent. Greeting Graden in a corset when he comes home after a long, hard day. Graden ripping lace off my body. His body covering mine while scraps of expensive lingerie litter the floor around our bed.

I catch his gaze and worry that he can see my thoughts. But other than his normal, intense stare, all seems okay.

Leslie the supermodel shopgirl smiles at him. "You two just made my day. This is my favorite part of the job. I always wanted to be a personal shopper. We have some things you will both love." She shoos Graden over to the little couch set up for waiting and pulls me into a beautiful dressing room in the back, snagging a clipboard and tape measure on our way.

I'm trying so hard to be cool, but I think I might burst into tears. She's going to want to undress me to measure me and bring me things to try on. How can I expose myself to her when she's so perfect and I'm so very not?

"Hey," she says, noticing my reticence. "What's wrong?"

I look around the posh room made to look like a fancy boudoir. If this were really my life, it would be perfect. But I don't have a fancy boudoir body, and the man waiting for me isn't my boyfriend. And it isn't fair that Leslie is so beautiful *and* nice. I exhale. "I wish you were about twenty years older and a size twenty-two instead of two," I admit, skipping the rest.

"Oh, honey, no." She sits on the chaise and pulls me down next to her. "You are gorgeous. Stop comparing yourself to other people. You have awesome curves, and that man out there obviously thinks so, too."

"We're not...we're not really a thing. He's not my boyfriend, really."

Her perfectly arched eyebrows raise. "Maybe not yet, but my gosh, the way he looks at you made me feel butterflies."

She's nice. Doesn't look crazy. Doesn't seem stupid. And probably has way more experience with men than I have, but there's no way she's right about that. "How did he look at me?"

"Like he wanted to drag you into his cave. Seriously, I think he's got it bad for you."

I shake my head. "He thinks of me like a sister."

She purses her lips and shakes her head like I'm the one with a screw loose. "No, honey. No, he doesn't." She stands up, dragging me with her. "Let's get you down to your panties and bra so I can get you some measurements. Then you are going to spend an obscene amount of money on scraps of lace to decorate that man's cave floor. Believe me, we are going to bring him to his knees."

Chapter Five

GRADEN

We've been in this shop for a long ass time.

When the salesclerk, Leslie, joins me on the couch, I'm prepared for her to hit on me, despite her thinking I'm here with my girlfriend. Something about me seems to attract the kind of woman who doesn't care. But instead, Leslie pats my knee in a very nonsexual way. "I think Rebecca needs your advice."

"My advice? I don't know anything about lingerie. That's sort of your department."

"Maybe advice is the wrong word. I think she needs encouragement. She's feeling a little...well, she just needs her man in there for a minute to build her up. She looks amazing."

My whole body flushes hot at the thought of going back there and into her dressing room. "I'm not sure your other customers would appreciate some guy going back there."

"This is our dead time. I can make sure nobody bugs you for at least fifteen minutes, if you know what I mean?"

I pull the collar of my T-shirt away from my neck because it feels like it's choking me. It's been bad enough knowing she was back there naked and putting on all the sexy clothes. But I never expected I'd get to see her in those sexy clothes. And now Leslie thinks I should bang her in public, too. "She's, ah...too shy for that." But the things I could do to her in fifteen minutes in a dressing room if she really were mine.

Leslie shakes her head. "She needs you, Graden. Go to her. Make her feel good." She taps her watch. "Just try to keep the volume down."

I don't want to embarrass Rebecca by opting out of the boyfriend role and telling Leslie the truth. I knew Rebecca was feeling unsure of herself when we came in, which is why I pretended we were together in the first place. Backing out now, when I know she's feeling less than confident, according to Leslie, would do more damage, so I get up.

The walk to the dressing room feels like the Green Mile, and I'm already getting hard thinking what I might find in that room. I cough lightly and tap on the door. "Becks? Uh, Leslie sent me back here. You need anything?"

She opens the door and my heart stops.

So much skin. So much soft skin.

She pulls me in by my wrist and leans against the door after she closes it like she's blocking the world out. It makes the room feel more intimate knowing she wants me on this side of the door. With her and not with them on the outside.

She bites the corner of her lip and shrugs. "Leslie means well. She thinks we're really *together*, so...I didn't know how to tell her not to drag you back here. I'm sorry."

"Don't be sorry." There isn't anywhere else I'd rather be right now.

She gives me this impish smile, and I try to keep my eyes there, where she's quirking her lips, but holy fuck. The little lacy thing she's got on draws my eyes to her tits like neon arrows are pointing to them. "What do you call that? What you're wearing?" *And can you wear it every day?*

She does a little twirl. "It's a baby doll chemise. It's gorgeous, isn't it? I told her I was only buying underwear and bras today, but she practically forced me to try this on. Do you like it? I can't exactly wear it on a date underneath my clothes, so I'm thinking I'll have to save this outfit for *after* successful third dates, yeah? Fourth date outfit?"

I swallow back the words that would tell her *the hell* she's wearing it for another guy. It's sexy. More than sexy. Dirty but sweet as fuck. It's mostly sheer and black, but the cups around her tits are pink lace.

And when she twirled, I noticed it was mostly backless below the bra strap. Like an apron showcasing a sweet little thong. Fuck—a sweet little black thong with a pink bow.

"It's pretty," I manage to say, instead of the things I want. And it strikes me as odd that she showed me the back. Normally, she's shyer. Is she putting on a confidence she doesn't feel? Fake it 'til you make it kind of thing? Or did she really want me to see her?

She's watching me very carefully. I can't fuck this up. I don't want her to believe that I don't think she's gorgeous and sexy—but I'm afraid I'll give myself away if I elaborate.

I'm not conveying the right things with my eyes, though. She gets this disappointed look on her face like I just kicked her dog. "I should have Leslie put it back. It's not for me. Thanks for being a good sport."

Oh, Jesus. She's blushing the prettiest shade of pink, and I can see how low it goes now that she's mostly unclothed. I find my voice, but it's deeper than usual. Like I swallowed gravel. "It would be a crime to put it back. That lingerie was made for you."

She's trying to read me. She looks vulnerable and hopeful at the same time. "Yeah?"

I nod and put my hands in my back pockets to keep them from reaching for her. Then I realize that my dick is pressing against my zipper, so I sit down to cover that fucker from her gaze. "Yeah."

She turns to face the mirror, and I have an excellent view of the back again. That luscious ass is killing me. I wouldn't even have to undress her all the way. I could take her against the mirror, press her tits against the glass, and shove the panties to the side while I stroke my cock in her tight heat.

Not doing myself any favors here.

"Leslie thinks we're in love," she says, snagging my gaze in the mirror. "She said we look great together."

"You'd look great with anyone, babe. You're beautiful."

I feel like she's upset. She doesn't actually wish we were together, does she?

No, man. She doesn't. I'm just thinking with my cock. Trying to justify the way I want her.

"So, I'll buy this for the guys who pass the third date then."

The *guys*? Plural?

She fingers the hem, causing me to think about yanking it off her. She's still got my gaze locked with hers like a tractor beam from *Star Trek*. I'm not sure I have the kind of strength required to disengage. "Remember, I'm looking for a guy just like you, so you're saying this would make you hot, right? If you came to the condo for a romantic dinner, and I answered the door in this, you'd want me?"

She's making plans to seduce someone just like me in front of me. In my damn house. Can this get any more fucked up?

"I'd more than want you, sweetheart. I'd be on my knees worshipping you."

She gets that impish smile back. "Oh, I like the sound of that."

She moves her hand up to the scalloped edge of the front over the lace that frames her tits. "Just think, the next time I wear this, I won't be a virgin anymore. It's weird to think about, isn't it? I mean, I may not even know the man yet who sees this next."

Our eyes meet in the mirror again. This time, I see something calculating in her gaze. She's testing me. She's fucking testing me. Like the twirl.

Does she have some sort of killer instinct? Talking about other men getting to see this when I won't? Talking about a fourth date with the guy who takes her cherry who isn't me.

I stand up and take a step so that I'm directly behind her, but not touching her. Just a breath of space between us. Her sugary scent teases me, but her eyes are locked with mine in the reflection. The tension weighs down on us like the air before a storm breaks.

From the corner of my eye, I can see her chest moving rapidly, like she's breathing fast and shallow.

"You're perfect," I tell her. She starts to disagree, but I splay my hand over her soft abdomen and yank her against me, letting her feel how hard she's made me. She gasps. "Don't argue with me. When a man like me compliments you, you say 'thank you.'"

Her eyes go wide at my tone, but she whispers, "Thank you."

Yes. The beast inside likes the way she took to his dominant words.

And that's it. I'm fucking tired of fighting this. Fighting her. Fighting fate. Her whisper of submission just sealed her destiny to mine.

But I'll play her little game, if she wants.

"You really want to learn how to seduce a real man, baby?" My fingers flex and curl over the soft material covering her stomach. "You want me to teach you, teacher?"

She nods shyly, our gazes still locked in the mirror.

"You need to tell me then. Tell me what you want. I want to hear the words on your lips."

"I want—" she starts, but has to clear her throat. "I want you to teach me how to seduce a man like you, Graden. I want to know how to get a guy like you into my bed. How to keep him there." She might be shy, but I don't know if my assessment that she's naïve was right. It seems like she knows what buttons to push on me. "I want you to help me lose my virginity."

Her words are revving the engine inside me, getting me ready to take my foot off the brake and do what I've been dreaming of since I moved in with my sexy roommate. Her body is tempting me, all that sweet flesh begging to be marked by my callused hands, my stubble, my come. But it's her eyes that make me craziest right now. I could get lost forever in them. They're full of wonder and a little bit of fear.

I like that. Maybe I'm a dick for getting off on that. But I like that honeyed fear in her expression a little too much. I spent so many years protecting her, never knowing I'd be the biggest danger she faced.

She's trembling against me, sending little sparks up and down my body wherever we touch. She makes me burn so good, so hot.

I brush her hair off her neck and rest my chin on her shoulder, my other hand stroking down her arm leaving a trail of goose bumps wherever it sweeps across her skin. "If we do this, no more of this mall shit."

"Do what?" she asks.

"I'm going to teach you everything you need to break a man, sweetheart."

She arches her neck a bit, and I can't tell if it's a subconscious move or if she knows she's driving me crazy. But I can't resist and lick her skin. Her body tightens then goes slack, like I've turned her bones into Jell-O with the touch of my tongue.

I can't pull back the groan as it escapes my throat.

"I don't want to break a man, Graden. I want to marry one."

I swear I start leaking pre-come when she says that. Fuck. I should leave her alone. She wants a husband. A fucking groom. And the very thought should have me running back to the safety of an oil rig. But instead, it sets off a primal drumbeat in my heart that echoes through my whole body.

Marry. Husband. Groom. The words should be a mood killer to a man with no intention of ever getting shackled, but instead, I see an image of her in yards of white lace, and I want to fuck her more than I want to breathe.

"Break him first. Then you can do whatever the hell you want to him, and he won't fucking care."

She's got this serious look on her face, like she doesn't think she has the power. Like she doesn't have me wanting to tear out of my own skin because it's so tight on me. Constricting.

"What do I do first?" she asks.

"Look at yourself in the mirror. What do you see?"

She shrugs. "A girl in a pretty nightie."

No. That won't do. "That nightie is pretty because it's on you. Look at you." I run my hand from her shoulder to her wrist slowly, enjoying the silky slide of her skin under my palm. "Your skin is amazing. So soft. Lush."

"There's too much of it."

I grasp her arms roughly and pull her into me hard, my erection poking her, showing her with my body what is difficult for me to say. "The right guy won't be able to get enough. Look again." Her eyes take in the whole picture in the mirror. I can't hide my predatory gaze or the lead pipe in her back. "You're a fantasy. No man is worth your time. The one you give it to will be the luckiest man in the world."

It's going too far. Getting too close. There's no way she won't see everything I want to hide.

We hear voices getting closer, and I realize our fifteen minutes are nearly up.

She leans back further into me. "I promise I'll do whatever you say if you teach me how to seduce you."

"A man like me, you mean."

That blush paints her face and chest a beautiful pink. "Of course. A man *like* you."

I spin her around, holding her by the shoulders as she jerks her chin up. My mouth is about to go crashing into hers. I'm already anticipating the sweet flavors of her lips. I bend down, a trace of air between our mouths.

"Graden? Rebecca? My coworker's lunch is over, and the store is getting busy." Leslie's warning pierces the lusty thoughts I'm having, and I set Rebecca a foot away from me.

Rebecca stares at me for a second before answering Leslie. "Okay, thanks. We're...just about done. I'll send Graden out first."

The beast inside roars his displeasure, but it's for the best. I need to help her move on because I am not the kind of man she needs. She wants a groom. A husband. A life.

All I can offer her is a lot of going nowhere at top speed.

Chapter Six

REBECCA

After things got so heated in the dressing room, I wasn't sure what to expect. Graden was obviously not unaffected by the sight of me in that sexy chemise. Leslie had been right when she told me that. And she had been right telling me not to disclose that she knew we weren't a couple. To play along so he would make a move.

Except I feel really guilty that I kept that from him. That's so not me. Playing games. It doesn't help that I got what I wanted. I even think he would have kissed me if we had another thirty seconds of time before the interruption.

But Graden returned to normal by the time we got home. No more growly, domineering hot male. To my utter and complete disappointment.

Maybe just the sight of a woman in underwear created a normal reaction that any guy would have felt at the moment. And like all the other guys I've gone out with, once the moment was over, Graden moved on.

I'm forgettable that way.

I don't want to act like nothing happened, but my pride is insisting that I don't show him how much he affected me. I can't deal with the rejection and still live here in this house with him. So, I'll just pretend the rejection isn't happening. That nothing out of the ordinary is happening. We're just roommates. Friends.

I'll figure out my guy problems without him. It's what I should have done to begin with. No more fantasizing about the hot guy I live with. No more pretending he's mine. No more remembering how wet he made me in the dressing room. I had to buy that lingerie I tried on because I completely ruined it.

I put the finishing touches on my makeup and slide out of my room quietly, hoping he's still napping on the couch where I made him rest his foot after walking around the mall.

I smooth down the fabric of my blouse. I wanted to buy a couple more sexy outfits today, but we didn't shop any more after we left the lingerie store, so I'm making do with an outfit I already had in my closet. Usually, I use two more buttons, but I'm going for broke tonight. I have big boobs—I might as well use them.

I'm changing strategies. Instead of having Graden help me get to date number three with a man so I can sleep with him and lose my virginity, I decided to just go get laid tonight. Maybe once I cross first-time sex off my bucket list, I'll be able to concentrate on meeting someone with relationship qualities because my lack of experience won't be hanging over my head. I was wrong in thinking that it should mean something and to wait for the right guy. I think my virginity is holding me back. Someday, I'll have sex with someone I love, I hope. I still want to find my future husband, if such a man exists.

But tonight, I need to have sex with someone willing and able and not worry about what Future Rebecca wants. I have to stop hoping for what isn't going to happen with Graden, too.

"You're walking like Elmer Fudd when he was hunting wabbits." Graden's voice startles me as I'm reaching for the doorknob. "Are you sneaking out for a reason?"

Yes, I'm sneaking out because I didn't want to face him. So much for that plan.

I turn, holding my purse to my chest so he doesn't see the cleavage I'm sporting. "I wanted you to rest. I left a note for you on the fridge."

He stretches, his massive arms reaching into the air, and his heavily lidded eyes are so sleep-sexy that I wish I could curl up with him and join him in a nap. Or other bedtime activities. But no. Not going there.

Not thinking about that. Not anymore. Not after he treated me like a sex goddess in front of that mirror and then turned it off the minute we left the store.

It's humiliating, really.

"Where are you going?" he asks.

"Out."

He raises his eyebrows. So I lift my chin in defiance. I don't have to tell him where I'm going. He's not my keeper.

"You have a date or something?"

I'm tempted to tell him yes, just to see if he gets jealous. But I won't. We are done playing that game. "I'm going out with friends. I'll probably crash at Jenn's, so I'll see you tomorrow."

His demeanor changes. Tenses. His face goes stone cold. "What's going on?"

"Nothing."

"You're acting weird."

"I'm really not. Just going out. Wicket is playing at The Dive, and I've told you how much Jenn likes to watch her boyfriend's band play live."

He stands up, testing his foot. "You've told me Jenn likes to make sure nobody hits on her boyfriend at Wicket's shows."

I smile. "That too." We don't say anything for a beat too long, making it super awkward. I hate this, the way things feel weird between us. I wish I hadn't had a taste of what it feels like to be wanted by him. It makes the absence of it ache in my heart.

"You want me to give you a ride? I can pick you up so you don't need to worry about driving."

"No, that's okay. I'm meeting Jenn at her house, and she's driving tonight. I'll just crash there..." Or somewhere else, maybe, if all goes according to plan. It's harder to imagine going someplace with another man when Graden is right here in front of me. But that's why I have to do it. I can't keep pretending he's mine. He barely said two words to me before his nap. And now I dread whatever he might say because it obviously isn't what I want to hear. I need to let him go.

"About today..."

I hold my hand up. "It's okay. I understand."

"You do?"

I nod. "We got carried away. Playing like we were an item, the lingerie, the idea that someone thought we were getting it on in there. It would be hard not to get a little worked up in that situation." I'm doing a great job of holding in the tears because what I really want to do is dissolve into a puddle of them so I don't have to face this moment where I'm making it so easy for him to reject me without hurting my feelings. "No harm, no foul though, right?"

"Becks..."

"I have to go. I'll see you tomorrow. I took a casserole out of the freezer. You can just pop it in the oven."

"Becks..."

I pause, but he doesn't fill the silence. And that tells me what I need to know.

"Bye, Graden."

Chapter Seven

GRADEN

I don't even know what just happened but I know I don't like it. I hate it, as a matter of fact.

I screwed up today. I know what I want. I know what she wants. What I don't know is how to live with myself if we both get what we want. So instead, I acted like nothing happened in that dressing room, and now she thinks I don't want her. It might be easier if I didn't—but I sure as hell don't want her believing that she isn't desirable.

I'm doing pull-ups to kill time and work out some energy when my mind strays to what she's doing tonight. She was hiding something from me. As I conjure up the ways I think she might be reacting to being shut down from me after I worked her up, I don't like where my mind goes.

She isn't going out to keep her friend company tonight. She's going out to make bad decisions. I can feel it. I should have seen it in her eyes earlier.

Fuck. I never should have come on to her in the dressing room. But I did. I was like some asshole staking a claim to her, and then I let her dangle in the wind not knowing where she stood. I'm the worst kind of jerk. She deserves so much better than me.

And I think she's going to go looking for it tonight.

Maybe that would be best.

But what if she's too upset and not thinking clearly? What if she puts herself in a dangerous position to prove something to me?

Fucking Cameron. Why did he ask me to take care of her? He knew exactly how unsuited for the job I am. He had to know he couldn't trust me with his baby sister. He would kick my ass if he saw how I treated her. He'd slit my throat if he could see my thoughts about her.

Fucking Cameron, why'd you have to die?

I shower. I eat. I try to watch a game. I find my keys. I drive to the bar. I curse myself the whole way.

She's the first thing I see when my eyes adjust to the dim interior at The Dive. There's very little light in the joint, but what there is attaches to her, singling her out to me. She's the prettiest girl I've ever seen. I've never been in over my head with a woman before. But I'm drowning in her. I don't even want to be rescued.

She's talking to some punk. His hand is pretty close to her drink, and I'm worried that he thinks he's going to put something in it. She's paying attention, though, and slides her hand over the top of the glass while she's pretend-laughing at something he says.

I know her real laugh, her real smile. And that ain't it.

I move through the crowd with her in my sights. My heartbeat is loud in my ears. She's my prey, and I'm a goddamned hunter. I don't think I can stop this now. That beast is back, and he won't be satisfied until she's ours.

As I get closer, I notice how low her shirt buttons start, and I know I'm not the only one appreciating the peekaboo of her bra. I was right. She is looking for trouble tonight. I guess she's going to find it.

I'm going to give her a hell of a lot of trouble.

She senses me staring at her and looks up, her lips drawing into a shocked "O." She grabs her friend's arm to get her attention, and Jenn gets that same surprised look. The dude talking her up takes one look at me and moves away.

Good choice, motherfucker.

"Graden?" she says when I reach her.

"I'm taking you home." The words are raw, and I didn't mean to say them. That damn beast inside got control for a second.

She narrows those eyes that shoot dagger-glares at me. "I don't think so. I'm happy here. And you don't get to tell me what to do."

"That's not what you were thinking earlier today."

She sputters, and I don't blame her. What the hell is my problem?

Jenn grabs her arm. "Do you want me to call somebody?" she asks Rebecca, eyeing me nervously.

I'm glad she has a friend who worries about her. "You don't ever need to protect her from me."

She and Rebecca exchange an entire conversation using just their eyes, and then Jenn tells us she's going to go find her boyfriend.

After she leaves, Rebecca gives me a look that might work on her students, but doesn't do shit except get me hotter for her. I am on fucking fire. Then she downs her drink the way she probably learned in college.

She sets her empty glass on the bar behind her. "You should go. I want to stay here."

"Thought maybe we could have another lesson tonight." My words are meant to be light, but I know they don't sound like it. I'm thirty seconds away from throwing her over my shoulder and hauling her ass out of here.

She shakes her head like she's dismissing me. "I changed the course objectives."

"Oh yeah? What are they now?"

"I decided I don't need to get to date number three. A one-night stand to take the edge off is a better plan."

The air in my lungs freeze. I don't think she's bluffing. "You're just going to pick some random guy and get it over with then, huh?"

Rebecca shrugs. "It's not your problem. I'm sorry I dragged you into it."

"So, who's the lucky guy?" I look around. "Tell me is isn't the punk I scared off already."

I've never seen the mask she's wearing now. Tough girl. Tired of my shit. "I think I'll have better luck if you leave."

Like. Hell.

"Why don't you give me a dry run? Work out the kinks. Pretend I'm the guy. Show me how you're getting me in your bed."

She narrows her eyes. "You're being a real asshole, you know that?"

Yeah, baby. I know that.

"Just show me, Rebecca. You wanted my advice, remember? You wanted me to help you figure out what you were doing wrong."

She glances around, probably looking for a drink to throw in my face, but everyone around us is holding theirs and her glass is empty. With a sigh, she reaches out to me and straightens the collar of the flannel I'd thrown on. Then she gives me a little smile. "I bought a new perfume today. Tell me what you think," she says sort of breathlessly, bringing her wrist up to my nose.

When did she buy a new perfume? I sniff dutifully, and it seems like the same perfume she's been wearing that drives me nuts. It's a light scent, not particularly evocative. But it's sort of elusive. I can only ever get hints of it at home, and it makes my gut clench for a deeper pull of the scent.

As she brings her hand down, she skims the front of my shirt. "Well, do you like it?"

"I...yeah...sure." I don't know why I'm tongue-tied. Then she flips her hair, just a touch, and I realize I'm being bamboozled.

She slides her hand around my wrist and reads the time on my watch. "My, it's getting late." She bites her lip and stares at mine. "Luckily, tomorrow is Sunday and I don't have to do anything but lounge around in bed all day."

Now I'm picturing her sliding around in my sheets. And that's her plan. She's...she's flirting with me.

She lets go of my wrist and leans against the bar on her elbows, which thrusts her tits out. I step between her legs, lean down into her space without touching her. Without touching those tits sticking up, testing the barrier of the small buttons. "You pick out this lucky man yet?"

She looks around the room like she's bored and shrugs. "Maybe the guy in the red shirt down there." She's tilting her head to the end of the bar, but I don't bother looking.

"You don't want him."

"No?"

I shake my head. "No." My heart is beating a primal beat, and my blood is too hot. "You want me."

She bites that lip again. "A guy *like* you, remember?"

Her words, the echo of our conversation earlier, are like a bullet tearing its way through me. Reminding me how I treated her today. How no matter how hard I try, no matter what I do or don't do, I am going to hurt her.

My eyes move from that damn lip down to the column of her throat, where her pulse jumps like I'm touching her. To the cleavage she's not hiding. To the black lace peeking through. She bought that bra today. With me. And hell if she's wearing it home with some other man. The scene in front of the mirror plays out in my mind, and I'm hard. Maybe harder than I've ever been.

"We're going home. Now." Before I can't stop myself from taking her here, in this bar, in front of God and everyone. Because I want to mark her. Claim her. And I want everyone to know she's mine. "You're going to break me tonight, Rebecca. And I'm going to teach you how."

Chapter Eight

REBECCA

We don't speak much the whole way home. I don't want him to change his mind like he obviously had when we left the dressing room earlier today. But I also don't understand what happened to get him to come find me tonight.

He wants to teach me to break him. I'm not even sure I know what that means.

But I really, really want to find out.

When we pull into the driveway, he tells me to wait and he runs around to my side to open the door. Of course, he always tells me to wait so he can open my door, but I'm still touched every time.

We get into the house and are beset with uncomfortable silence. The kind that makes the ticking of the clock on the mantel sound like it's super loud. Before yesterday, we didn't ever have uncomfortable or awkward silences. It's sad. But if I went back in time, if I never told him I was a virgin or asked him for advice, then I never would have seen that hungry look in his eyes when he saw me in lingerie. I never would have watched him prowl through a crowded bar looking for me so he could bring me home.

Does he even know how that affected me? If he'd have said, "Come with me," it wouldn't have been such a big deal. But no..."We're going home," means more. At least it does to me. Home means something, doesn't it?

But I can see he's rethinking this already.

If he thinks he can just keep yanking me around, he's got another thing coming.

"What was it that made you come find me tonight?" I ask. "Was it that you wanted me, or you just don't want anyone else to have me?"

His jaw squares, and he presses his lips into a firm line. "I'm supposed to be teaching you how to seduce a man, aren't I? I can't do that if you're not here."

A red haze clouds my vision. "Oh, right. I see. So, are you going to teach me how to fuck and then send me back to The Dive? Is that how this works?" He winces. "You could have just left me there tonight. I'd have figured it out on my own. I'm a smart girl. College educated and all."

"I knew you were planning something rash. So I went there to stop you."

"Something rash?"

Whose voice was that? It couldn't have been mine. It sounded like it could have broken glass.

"Something rash," he repeats dully. But his body language is clear that he already regrets what might happen next. He doesn't want me—he wants to take care of me, maybe. He doesn't want me to sleep with someone else, certainly. But that's not the same. And it's not enough for me.

"I don't believe this." I toss my purse on the table by the door. "Fine. You did it. You stopped me. Thank you for saving me from myself. You've done your good deed. It's too bad you have to keep acting like you want to have sex with me to get me to do what you want—but you're a real trooper for sticking it out. Don't forget to take your pill. I'm going to bed."

Tomorrow, I will look for an apartment. This isn't going to work for me anymore. I can't keep letting my desire for Graden stop me from living my life, and I know I'll never give any other guy a real chance if I think there's even the smallest chance with Graden.

And there isn't. He won't let there be. I don't know why he's so conflicted. I'm sure he'd never tell me. I try hard to tell myself it's his problem and not an extension of my normal man issues. But it's hard. It's so damn hard not to take it personally that something about me seems to repel men even if they seem all in for a few minutes.

I swallow the ball of tears forming in my throat.

I make it halfway across the room when the steely band of Graden's arm reaches around me and pulls me into his chest. "I'm sorry, Becks. I'm sorry I keep screwing this up."

God. He is so big and strong behind my back. I melt into him even though I don't want to. I can't stop craving his touch. "I don't understand what you want, Graden. I don't think even you know."

"I know exactly what I want. I just don't feel like I should have it."

"Why?" I reach for his other hand, the one that isn't gripping me so hard into him, and bring it to my cheek. I press my face into it like a cat. "Why shouldn't you have what you want?"

I kiss his palm, and he gasps. The world spins as he turns me in his arms and walks me backward to the wall so quickly I don't think my feet touch the ground. I'm trapped between him and the wall. I feel helpless and I like it.

The expression on his face is one of near agony, though. "I don't deserve you, sweetheart. You're so good and sweet. I'm not the guy for you. The things I want to do to you..." He slams his eyes closed as a shiver wracks his body. "I want to defile you. Do you understand? Rough and raw and filthy, baby. That's how I want to take you."

His eyes open again, and the way he is looking at me is positively barbaric. All that masculine power directed at me is overwhelming. My pulse kicks up as a new need claws at me from the inside. I want him to take me. Possess me. I want all that potent male energy covering my body, filling me up.

He groans, and I blink out of my little trance just as his mouth kicks into a feral grin and he says, "You like that, don't you, baby?" He pushes me against the wall harder so I can feel his solid erection. It's really hard and really big. Really, really big. "Fuck. I bet you are wet right now." My face heats because he's right. I'm soaked. "I'm going to take that cherry tonight. I'm going to feel your hot, wet pussy clenching around my cock. I'm going to make you lose your fucking mind. Make you crave my dick like a drug. Maybe then you'll understand how much I fucking want you."

I whimper, the sound so full of longing I should be embarrassed, but I'm not. "Yes. Yes, please, Graden. I need you so much."

He buries his face in my hair and groans again. "You smell so good. I can't get enough of you. I bet you taste good, too. I bet I'm going to get addicted to the taste of your pussy."

I arch into him then, angling the best I can so his cock will rub against where I need him most. There are too many clothes between us, though, and I exhale a frustrated sound when the friction isn't enough.

"You getting greedy, sweetheart? You want my cock in you already?"

"Yes. Please."

He pulls back and looks into my eyes. "I haven't even kissed you yet." Despite the primal fire burning in his eyes, he seems to bank it when he runs his finger from my temple down my jaw so gently I am surprised I can feel it. "You're so soft and sweet."

He presses his lips to my temple, then follows the path his finger made with soft kisses. If he didn't have me pinned to the wall, I don't think my legs would hold me. The sweet kisses undo me in a way even his dirty talk didn't. They are reverent, adoring. That this is the same man who wants to defile me makes me the luckiest girl in the world right now. Because I want it all. I want his sweetness and I want his filthy, filthy passion. I want him to tear me apart and kiss me back together.

When he gets to my lips, he cups my jaw in those big, rough hands and takes small sips of my mouth like I'm a fine wine to be savored. I'm trying to be patient because these kisses are wonderful, but he's the spark to my tinder, and I know I'm about to burst into flames. I dart my tongue out for a taste of my own, and we combust around his untamed growl. He grinds his stiff cock into my belly and plunges his tongue into my mouth. And I take it. Oh God, do I take it. My fingernails are clawing at him, unable to get him close enough while his mouth is basically fucking mine.

Thinking I'm smart, I lower my hands to his hip, pulling him harder into me so I can grind on that hard erection that has my name on it. On a guttural groan that sounds like it was pulled out of him, he stops kissing me long enough to grab my hands, pinning them to the wall on either side of my head. "You are going to make me come in my jeans if you keep doing that."

"So take them off."

"I have plans for you, sweetheart. So you're just going to have to wait."

I struggle briefly to get control of my hands back but realize that just isn't going to happen. He's too strong. And he wants control right now. Which is delicious, if you ask me, so I stop struggling and cede to him. That fire flares in his eyes again when he feels me submit.

"Do whatever you want to me, Graden. I'm yours."

There's a moment of complete stillness between us—like the one before a jaguar leaps on its prey. Calmly, almost too carefully, he brings my wrists higher above my head and transfers them both to one hand. He cups the back of my neck in the other and brings himself to eye level with me. It's intense, unlike anything I've ever felt, when he looks so deeply into my eyes I feel like he's seeing straight into my soul.

My pulse is racing, and something wild inside me is unfurling, beating at my bones and skin to be let out. I've never felt this way before. I don't even know how to express it.

Graden swallows hard. "You're mine. You've been mine for a long time. I'm not going to fight it anymore, if this is what you want."

"Yes, yes, I want this."

"You need to be sure. Once I take you, sweetheart, I'm never giving you up. You'll belong to me completely. Forever."

"And you'll belong to me, Graden."

"Fuck, yeah, I will. God, that sounds so amazing." He leans his forehead on mine. "I feel like I've been fighting this so long, and I don't even remember why half the time."

If this is a dream, I don't want to wake up.

He's about to kiss me again, but I panic and whisper. "Wait...I need to tell you something."

He opens his eyes as he's still pressed against my forehead. He banks that fire...just barely. "What is it, sweetheart?"

The intimacy of our closeness and the way we are both whispering makes it easier. Not a lot easier, but some. "Today, in the dressing room, I set you up. Please don't be mad. Leslie already knew you were just pretending to be my boyfriend. It was her idea to send you back there to see how you reacted. And I shouldn't have gone along with it. It was dishonest."

Graden smiles.

"You're not mad?"

He kisses the bridge of my nose. "I love how honest you are. You never had to tell me, but you did."

"I don't want anything between us. I don't like to play games."

He thinks about that for a minute. "Why'd you go along with her idea?"

Because I'm so lame. "I wanted to see if she was right. If you would like seeing me in the lingerie. If you were attracted to me."

"I did. I am."

I feel so much better now with the air cleared between us. "Okay, then kiss me again."

And he does. He brings me back to boiling so fast with his kisses.

He's moved those lips to my neck. I had no idea it was such an erogenous zone on me, but I can't stop rocking my hips. He's breathing hard, like he's fighting to contain himself. But I want him wild. "Graden—I know why I waited." I clutch his hair, bringing his gaze back to my face. "I'm still a virgin because I was waiting for you. All this time, it was you."

I see the change. If he were some kind of supernatural creature, his fur would have come out or his fangs would have popped. Instead, he growls and yanks the front of my shirt down hard, tearing fabric and sending buttons skittering across the carpet. He sucks one of my nipples through the bra, and my body arches, my back bowing as I hear a high keening noise and realize it's me.

He grunts again and pulls my bra down, releasing my breasts to spill out of the cups. "You're mine," he tells me as he starts suckling, sending sparks shooting through my whole body. "Tell me. Say it."

I can hardly catch my breath, but I say, "I'm yours. Yes. All yours."

I've had guys touch my boobs before. But it was nothing like this. I know they are big—after all, they go with the rest of me and nothing about me is petite. But they usually make me self-conscious. But with Graden being in total awe and in worship-mode, I'm finally happy to say they are not too big. He can't get enough, and suddenly I feel at home and happy with my body. It was made for him. For me. For us. I've seen the way women look at him and know he could have any of them he wants. But he is making it clear to me that he wants me.

And he's wanted me for a while. Whatever rejection I was feeling wasn't about him not desiring me. Knowing Graden, he probably thinks he's not good enough for me. Or he's got some sense of honor that says he can't mess with his friend's little sister. But knowing that he's this hot for me, for my body, frees me in a way I've never felt.

I finally understand the power I have. He told me I could break a man like him. He probably didn't know I could put him back together, too.

I try to move my hands so I can touch him, but he's still got a pretty strong hold on me. "Do you like this, sweetheart? Do you like it when I suck on your big tits? Is it making you wet?"

"Everything about you makes me wet, Graden. Go ahead and check."

He gives me that feral grin again and bites my nipple. The shock of pain followed by the soothing lick of his tongue makes me cry out.

"Yes, oh God, yes!"

"You're my dirty little teacher, aren't you? All sweet words and cookies by day, and fucking hot pussy by night. I'm going to learn all your secrets, baby. I'm going to master everything that makes you writhe and cry out in pleasure. I don't think you're ever going to get a full night's sleep again."

My legs are weakening with every syllable he utters. He undoes my jeans and snakes his hand down my pants.

"Fuck, you're soaked. Such a good girl, getting ready for me." When he pulls his hand out and licks me off his fingers, I almost pass out I'm so turned on. "Jesus, you taste good. So good. I'll never get enough of you."

"Take me to bed, Graden," I plead while I try to kick off my boots.

"We haven't been on three dates yet, Becks. Don't you want to wait?" he teases even as we both groan at the contact and friction between our jeans while I try to maneuver the boots off.

"I don't want to wait." I reach up and suck on the skin under his jaw. "I want you to make me a woman. I want to give you everything. Nobody's ever touched my pussy before, Graden." The guttural sound he emits gives me confidence that I've got him where I want him now. "You'll be the first."

"I'll be your fucking last." He yanks my pants down, taking the pretty new underwear I'd bought today with them. As I step out of the legs, he drops to his knees and plants his face between my legs, inhaling deeply. I'm not used to this kind of raw intimacy, and I freeze up a little.

He presses his cheek to the spot just above my pussy and looks up at me. "It's all right, baby girl. Just relax. I'm going to eat your sweet pussy, baby, until my tongue is your whole world and you forget your own name. And then I'm going to eat it some more. Give me five minutes, and you'll never be shy with me again."

Well, I don't know about that, but I'm certainly willing to give him a shot. I stroke his hair while he's looking up at me. It's soft like silk, so strange on a man who's hard all over. He grabs my hand and kisses it.

He's like a god on his knees in front of me. Me! A pudgy, slightly frigid schoolteacher. And he's smelling my pussy like we're animals and kissing my fingers like I'm a queen. I don't know how to deal with all these different sides of him, but when he rises up and sweeps me into his arms, it doesn't matter.

And holy shit. He's carrying me like I weigh nothing.

And then I'm in the middle of my bed, and he's taking my blouse and bra all the way off. And then comes his shirt.

I was laying back on the pillows, but I rise up to get me some of that. I want to touch all of him. He's so gorgeously made. Part giant maybe. Muscles honed by honest, hard work. Powerful, strong. I can't wait to feel the weight of him on top of me. I want to be surrounded by all that strength.

"Pants, Graden. Take off your pants."

He stands up, his hand on the top button near the bulge straining the zipper. And then he shakes his head. "No."

Chapter Nine

GRADEN

Rebecca is on her knees in the middle of the bed and I want to fuck her so hard that the bed breaks beneath us. But I'm not going to.

Not yet.

I can't take my pants off. I've gotten this far without really thinking of the logistics. In all my fantasies, it was never a problem. But I never thought we'd really get this far.

If I take off my pants, I'm going to scare the shit out of her.

I'm a big man. All the fuck over. One woman uttered, "Urban legend," when she first saw me. I don't brag because I was born like this and didn't do anything to earn it. And having a monster cock isn't always an advantage. I got teased some in the locker room, but that part was never a big deal. Some women seem to be excited about it...at first. But it's sometimes a lot of work and sometimes, well, women give up.

And occasionally, I've been told it hurts too much to try.

I know it fits. I mean... it looks like it won't at first, but it *will* fit. If the woman is relaxed and lubricated enough. The girl staring at me is dripping wet. But she's a virgin. I've stayed far away from virgins in the past. For obvious reasons.

I don't want to hurt her. I'd kill for her. I'd die for her. I don't want to be the one who hurts her.

But I want her. I need to make her mine. But the idea of causing her pain almost makes me wish I could go soft and we could just cuddle all night.

But that isn't going to happen. The beast in my pants is ready to own her. The best I can do is go slow and keep her coming enough to be distracted.

"Lay down, baby. Show me that pussy." My voice comes out thick.

My sweet schoolteacher looks disappointed that my jeans are still on, but she'll get over it. She reclines all the way and opens her legs.

"Your pussy is the sweetest thing I've ever seen." I get on the bed, my jeans too tight to move easily, and spread her legs further so I can get between them. I lift one, straightening it, and bring my mouth to the inside of her ankle, pressing soft, moist kisses there while I stroke up and down her leg. "Your body was made for me. You turn me on so much."

I move up her leg slowly. She's soft and smooth everywhere, and when I finish exploring one leg, I start on the other. The bedspread beneath her ass is damp, just the way I want it, so I keep working her slow, keeping her wet and ready. She's got a spot behind her knee that makes her whole body shiver, so I explore there, experimenting with patterns and pressure until she brings her hands up to those gorgeous tits like she can't stop herself from playing. That's so sexy. I have to unbutton my jeans or they will cut off circulation.

I move around her body, skipping where I want to be the most to massage her arms. When I get back to her irresistible stomach, her hands automatically cover it. I ease them to her sides, uncovering her body to me again. But she tilts her chin and won't look right at me.

"Hey," I say, hoping my voice is soothing. "What's going on?"

"Nothing, sorry. I just...got weird for a second."

I touch her stomach again and she jerks. I palm her belly, rubbing it gently. "I love your body, Becks. All of it. You don't get to cover up or hide parts of you from me. You're mine."

She rolls her eyes. "I didn't mean to bring insecurities in here. It just hit me for a second. You don't have to make me feel better."

I kiss her tummy, bite it, suck it the same way I'd done to her tits earlier. "I fucking love your stomach. I think it's sexy as hell. It's not anything you should be insecure about. I've been dying to touch every part of you. Your curves make me hot."

"Do you usually date overweight women?"

"No. I don't usually *date* anyone. You're the first woman I've gotten to know and like before we had sex. I don't do relationships. But if you're asking if I have a fetish or I'm a chubby chaser, then no. I've never had any certain *type* of woman before." I can't tell if I'm making it better or worse at this point. "Rebecca, your body makes me hot because it's you. The way you laugh makes me hot. The way you sing when you don't know you're doing it makes me hot. The way you cook food and play Candy Crush and water plants makes me hot. I want to touch you all the time. It's not because you have big tits, but your big tits make me hard. And your soft belly and your warm thighs...all of you." I move up her body and kiss her. "Wait until you hear the things I want you to do with that heart-shaped mouth."

She raises up on her elbows, looking confident again. "Why are you still wearing pants?"

Because my gigantic dick is going to scare the fuck out of you.

"If my cock comes out, it'll be over too soon. I want to eat you." I push her shoulder gently so she lays back down. I wasn't lying. I'm extremely turned on by her softness, the squishy parts of her body make me want to squeeze her. It's true that most of the chicks I've banged have been skinnier, but if Rebecca tries to go on a diet or starts hiding her body from me, we'll have words. I want her the way she is. Jiggling is no crime.

I need to get her back out of her head, and so far, dirty talk makes her cream, so I go back to what works. "Rebecca?"

"Yeah."

"Lay down and show me your cunt. I want to see how fucking wet your little slit is."

Her eyes go round from shock, but her pupils dilate, letting me know that rough talk turned her on and the last thing on her mind is the little jiggle in that tummy.

I use her own hand to dip into her pussy, and then I suck the juices off her fingers. "You're so sweet." I want in that pussy, but I've been neglecting her big breasts too long, so I draw some of her wetness onto my fingers and paint her nipples with my hand. Her eyes get big, wondering what dirty thing I'm going to do to her next as I move up her body and start sucking the sweet cream off the berry-sized nip. I'm making noises I can't control anymore as I continue to play with her and use her juices on her tits. She's bouncing around, unable to keep her hips still. I stuff as much tit in my mouth as I can, like a glutton, pulling it deep into my mouth and moaning around it. She's so fucking perfect. I love the way she tastes, the sounds she makes. I bring my hand down, and she uses hers to hold it there. I think she's close, so I press the heel of my hand over her clit and suck that nip into my mouth hard.

"Oh God. Oh God. You're going to make me come." I keep pressing and dip my fingers into her hole, holding them there as she stretches around them.

"Come on my hand, baby. I want you to get off on me. Such a dirty teacher." I bite down like I did in the living room, and she cries out my name, falling into her orgasm so prettily. "That's it, sweetheart. You're so beautiful when you come. I'm never going to get tired of watching you do that."

She's shivering a little, so I lay on top of her and roll us over so she's resting her head on my chest while she comes down from her high.

My cock is fucking aching. I'm probably going to blow a load in my pants because I can't keep this up. I still want to eat that pussy, though.

When she's breathing right again, I slide back down to paradise and give her a few slow licks. She's wet, so damned wet. It's the most erotic feeling, all slick and warm on my tongue. I want to cover my face in her girl juice like it's a glaze. I love the way she smells and tastes.

I leave her clit alone for a few more minutes, knowing she's sensitive, but I get my tongue everywhere else. I spread her legs as wide as I can and bury my tongue in her virgin hole. She's tight, and I'm worried again about hurting her. It's never far from my mind. She starts making those pretty sounds again, so I use my tongue like it's my dick and fuck her, getting as deep as I can.

Mine. She's all mine.

I can't stop thinking about how I'm going to be the first one in there. The last one, too. There's no way another man is ever getting near her. Not now. When her hands move to my hair, clutching me to her, I know I can get back to the pretty little clit.

I can't get enough. I suck her lips and her clit, savoring her like a peach. I want to devour her, and I bury my face in that sweet, sticky cunt. She starts grinding on my face, and so I grab her ass and hold her to me as hard as I can, probably leaving marks on her butt as she starts coming like a freight train, bearing down and calling out my name.

She's wrung out now. As relaxed as she'll ever be, so that's when I ease off her and finish taking off my pants. When I get back on the bed, she opens her eyes lazily, and then sits up like she's seen an intruder.

"Oh my God," she says. Her eyes get bigger and her face loses color. "You're..."

I look down at my Johnson. "Big. Yeah."

She blinks rapidly. "That is not big. That is gigantic."

Fuck.

"You're gonna have to make friends, Becks, or this isn't going to work."

"Okay, okay. Just give me a second to process this." She tears her eyes away from it to my face. "How...big...is?"

"Big enough." I don't know how to tell her that it's actually gotten a little softer since she started freaking out. I want to fuck her so bad, but I can't deal with hurting her. I don't see how I can not do one or the other. "Do you trust me?"

"Of course I do."

"Do you still want to do this?"

Her eyes meet mine, and then she launches herself across the bed and into my arms. "Graden, you're all I want. Yes, I want you to fuck me. I promise."

My arms wrap around her. "You're not scared." She feels so good pressed against me, skin on skin.

"Of course I'm scared. But I know you'll make it good for me. I trust you. And I believe in you."

Chapter Ten

REBECCA

That was the right thing to say.

Graden's arms tighten around me, and he takes my mouth in a possessive, feral kiss. I melt into him, knowing where I belong even if it all feels so strange and uncertain to me. I've spent years feeling like there was something wrong with me, and then the hottest guy I could dream up has spent the last hour focusing on my pleasure. Telling me he wants me. Telling me the parts of me that I think are ugly are beautiful to him.

And now, I find out he's got the blue ribbon of all cocks. His is not a starter penis. And right now, it's pushing against my stomach as he kisses me. And the tingles start in my core again, even though the thought of having him inside me is more than a little scary.

The kiss is getting more possessive. More dark and raw, and I feel an answering need inside when he wraps my hair around his hand and tugs hard. The sharp sting with the deep kiss turns my blood to fire. I'm going to fly out of my skin and shoot like a star into the universe. Graden's mouth moves lower, sliding up and down my throat. I want him to bite me, mark me.

"You're so fucking mine," he murmurs, nipping at my neck.

I'm coming alive again. This man and his dirty words and his need for me that he doesn't hide overwhelm my senses. His hands go lower and he squeezes my ass cheeks roughly. An hour ago, I would have been worried my butt was too big and jiggly. But now, the more he touches it, the more he grunts like a caveman, the more I'm glad my body is the way it is.

"Such a juicy ass, baby. Made for my hands. I can't fucking get enough of you."

And then I am laying down, and he is on top of me. We are skin-to-skin touching from head to toe, and that big cock is sliding between our stomachs, catching the moisture between my legs and spreading it around. "You feel so good, Graden. I love the weight of you on top of me."

He pauses and looks deeply into my eyes. Everything becomes so clear to me. He's been saying I'm his in that possessive way, but it isn't until this moment that I understand what that means. I mean, it's been hot to hear, and it turns me on when he's all dominating and alpha male with me, but it's now, naked in this bed, looking into his eyes, that I finally *get* it.

Yes, I'm his.

I belong to him. I belong *with* him.

And he belongs to *me*.

"Graden."

"Yeah, baby?"

"I can't wait to feel you inside me. I want you to show me everything. Show me how it feels to belong to you."

He rests his head on my chest. "Fuck. I need you so much, but I don't want to hurt you."

I move my hips, sliding that cock between us. "I trust you. You'll make it good. You'll take care of me."

He shudders like the feeling is too much and returns his gaze to mine.

"Graden, I love you."

He makes a low sound in his throat, and all his muscles tighten and bulge. He is so masculine, so virile. He's everything. My world narrows until it's just him.

"I can't resist you."

He pulls back and grasps that huge cock. It's intimidating for sure, but when he starts sliding it around my mound, dipping it between the lips of my pussy, and tapping it against my clit, I moan with pleasure.

"I'm going to make you come so hard with this beast, baby. You'll be my little cock slave, willing to do anything I say to get this back in you."

It's so heavy and perfect. "Yes, anything you want."

Show me how to break you, Graden.

It is time to make friends with that beast, so I reach for it. I can't get my hand around the whole thing, of course, but I stroke it slowly and watch his eyes go heavy-lidded with pleasure.

His cock is wet from me and smooth like velvet. I don't know what I thought it would feel like, but the texture makes me want to rub it all over my body. I move it against my pussy, and we both hiss in ecstasy. "I can feel you getting harder. How is that even possible?"

"It's all you, sweetheart. You're so sexy. Pure and filthy at the same time. You make me feel like an animal. You make me want to do things..." he breaks off when I pay attention to the crown of his dick with my hand. I make note of that for later. The ridge where he's most sensitive is all mine now.

But I still don't feel like I know what happens next. Well, I do...but I don't. This is so much further than I've ever gone. I don't want to make some stupid blunder and ruin it. "What things do you want to do to me? Tell me."

"You want me to shock you, sweetheart? Tell you all the dirty things I'm going to do to all your holes? Oh yeah, that one too, honey."

Oh my God. I nod and rub the mushroom head all around my pussy. "Yes, tell me. Please." I arch involuntarily at the sensation of that heavy cock on my clit.

"There isn't a part of you that won't belong to me. Be marked by me. I'm going to come inside you, fill you up with all my come. My balls are heavy with it. Making so much of it to put in you."

He covers my hand with his, and we stroke him together. When he taps that crown on my clit again, I come apart. It's almost embarrassing how hard I come, like he's tasering me with that cock or something. But he doesn't seem to think it's bad.

"Oh fuck, yeah. Baby, that's so hot how you come for me. I love when you surrender yourself to me completely."

I'm still coming down when he notches himself at my opening. I try not to tense up. I know it will fit. If a baby can come out of me, this man can get into me.

Baby. Crap.

"Wait." I still him with a hand on his wrist.

He looks concerned. "You scared? You want to stop."

I shake my head. "No. I just remembered we're not using any birth control."

"You're not on the pill?"

I shake my head again. "It makes me sick. I have condoms...but..." I lift my head and look at the baseball bat between his legs. "There is no way they would fit you."

He smiles, pleased, I think, that he has this problem. "I have condoms in my room." He looks down where his cock rests in my pussy. "I get tested every six months. I haven't been with anyone for longer than that."

I try not to act too surprised. But wow. I really am. He's the kind of guy who is in hot demand. Plus, his libido seems pretty high. I can't imagine him going without that long. But then, I haven't seen him going out of his way to go out and get laid since we've been living together. I guess I just assumed.

Now that I'm more accustomed to him, he's starting to feel really good inside me. I know it's just the tip, but I like it. It's not responsible to keep going. I know it. He knows it. But neither of us say anything. He pushes in just a little more, stretching me. I don't ask him to stop. Another inch goes in. My heartrate jacks up.

His temples are sweaty, and his arms are tense from holding back. He's not pulling out. He's not going all in. We're in this weird limbo. My inner muscles clench around him, and we both make low noises in our throats. It feels so good. Too good. "What are we doing, sweetheart?"

"It's wrong, but I don't want you to pull out right now," I say honestly. "I don't want you to wear a condom. I want to feel you. All of you, with nothing between us."

He actually starts shaking. "You keep talking like that and I'm going to turn into a rutting animal. I'm just a man, sugar. I can only resist temptation so long before I take what you are offering."

It's crazy. I know it is. We're looking into each other's eyes, and I can see his thoughts, and I know he reads mine too. Me pregnant with his baby. Big and round. Fertile. Carrying the evidence for everyone to see what we did. It's wrong, and it's so hot it makes me crazy with need. We can't. We shouldn't.

We want to.

"Fuck." He pushes a little more and meets the resistance of my hymen. This is it. We both know it. "Baby, tell me to stop. Tell me to go get a condom. Don't let me do this. The only way I'm pulling out right now is if you tell me to. But I will if you ask me to."

I place my hand over his heart. It's beating so hard. I know he would never put me at risk; I believe him that he's clean. And I know he would never abandon me or a child we make, even if this is just a one-time thing.

And a baby isn't the worst thing. If I'm being honest, I want to be pregnant. I want to be a mom. It's not the right time, maybe. But I could never regret it.

"I don't want you to pull out."

His big hand covers more than half my face as he holds me still to take his kiss. Like I'd try to get away. His hold is possessive, and his tongue pushes into my mouth obscenely. He's fucking my mouth when he breaches my virginity, pushing right through it on one solid thrust, absorbing my shocked gasp in his mouth. I freeze up and then my instincts make me try to push him away, but he holds me still. I'm pinned to the bed by his dick, his hand holding my face to his, forcing me to take his kisses while my body adjusts to the intrusion.

"Breathe, angel."

"It hurts."

"I know, sweetheart. Just give it a minute, okay. Trust me?"

"Always."

"Oh baby, you don't know what that does to me. I love that you just keep giving me that sweet trust. I'll make it good. Don't worry. Just try to breathe and relax for a minute."

He kisses me again, and I concentrate on the way he tastes. The way his tongue feels against mine. My chest loosens up, and I can breathe again. I still feel incredibly full. Almost too full, but the sting is starting to ease, and when he shifts, we both gasp at the intense feeling.

"You're so tight. Feels so good. Are you doing okay, sweetheart?" He thrust a little more.

My fingernails gouge his shoulder. "Oh, yes. More."

"You sure?"

I nod. "More," I assure him.

"Baby, open your eyes and look at me."

I hadn't realized they were closed. I blink up at him. He looks concerned, but underneath there's this level of...ferocious is the only word I can think of. "I'm not all the way in. Do you understand? There's more."

"Oh. *Oh*." Good God. How big is this man? He still looks fierce, his face a mask of an angry warrior. "Are you mad at me?"

He relaxes his expression with what looks like great concentration. "No. Your pussy is just tighter than anything I've ever felt. You're squeezing me so good. It's taking every ounce of control I have not to force you to take all of it. I want my cock in you to the hilt." He's gritting his teeth, forcing himself to go slow. "I want to impale you on it."

"Do it." He closes his eyes, still fighting his hunger. "Do you want me to beg?" He grunts. Well, I'm not above begging, not if it gets us what we both want.

I wrap my legs around him for more leverage, but I can't force him in the way he's holding himself. He's too strong. But I have a hunger, too. I want that cock. Bad. He may have fallen for a shy schoolteacher, but the woman he just made wants all of him. She won't be denied.

"Graden, I want you to make me your little slut. I need it, baby. Make me yours. Give me all that cock. Please. I'm begging you."

"Jesus Christ, you're killing me." He was no longer staying still, but his shallow thrusts weren't enough. Not for him. Not for me.

"Graden, I love knowing we're doing this raw." He groans. "I love knowing when you come, you're going to fill me up. I can't wait to feel you gush inside—"

He shuts me up with a deep kiss, but it's almost playful. Heaven knows we're enjoying ourselves.

"That's not fair," I tell him when he lets me up for air.

"You're not playing fair. Talking dirty. Trying to make me come."

"I don't know why you're fighting this so much."

He rests his forehead against mine. "I don't want it to be over."

"Graden, it doesn't ever have to be over."

A pained look flashes across his face, and then he looks oddly peaceful. Like my words just sank in, and he has a new understanding. "I love you, Rebecca," he says. "I'm done fighting it. You said you loved me, and I hope you meant it because you're mine now. I'm going to take care of you and keep you so satisfied, you'll never even think about what you might be missing out on." He thrusts all the way in, hard. "And I'm putting a fucking baby in you tonight."

The action shocks me as I make sense of his words. And then nothing makes sense and all I can do is feel.

Chapter Eleven

GRADEN

I'm a fucking animal, and it's all her fault. She did this, and I hope she's happy because I am not going to stop until there's so much of me leaking out of her that it will still be coming out tomorrow.

Her heels dig into my ass and I let go, pistoning inside my woman, while my hands grab whatever flesh I can. Jesus, I'm possessed. She's just so soft, cushioning me as I slap against her. Nothing has ever felt so good. So right.

She's taking my cock like a champ. I know it's too much. Too big. I should slow down and go easy on that poor cunt of hers. But it feels so good, like it's trying to squeeze the come out of me, her inner muscles clenching me tight.

I'm leaking so much pre-come I can actually feel it coming out, mixing with her juices, coating the walls of her virgin pussy. Goddamn. She's not a virgin anymore, though. She's mine.

"Are you going to make me pregnant?' she asks.

I want to. God, the thought of her swollen belly and milk-filled tits makes me pump harder. It's too soon. We shouldn't be taking this kind of risk. I never even thought about being a father before her. But if I thought I was horny a few minutes ago, it's nothing compared to the idea of knocking her up. "You want my come, sweetheart?" I hold still, feeling like my entire life is hanging in the balance waiting for her answer. "You want me to make you pregnant. Make you a momma?"

She starts gushing hot honey around my cock, her pussy pulsing wildly, milking me for sperm. "Yes, yes, please give me your baby."

That's when I can't control the beast any longer. I shove it into her like a battering ram on a castle door. The headboard is banging into the wall. She's still coming around me, still crying out my name, lost in her pleasure. We're sloppy wet, the slurping sounds when I rut in and out of her are obscene.

"Take. All. Of. It." I slam into her with one final thrust and pour into her. The sensation sends her into another climax, her inner muscles pulling more seed out of me than should be possible.

I'm not just ejaculating, I'm letting go of everything I've held inside. I'm giving her everything I am, and everything I want to be. I roll to my side, but don't pull out of her. I'm not ready to let her go.

"Are you okay?" Please be okay.

"More than okay. Is it always like that? I've been missing out on so much."

"No, baby. It's not always like that." It's never like that. At least not in my experience. "That was special. You're special."

"Maybe we're special."

She looks well and truly fucked, but happy. And I'm fucking smiling. I'm...happy too.

Chapter Twelve

REBECCA

It's been three days since our first time and I'm sore. Really sore. But I seem to forget that every time I see that hungry look in his eyes. Which is a lot. He's a man with an appetite.

We're snuggled on the couch, my back to his front.

His gigantic hand is rubbing circles on my belly, and it feels better than nice. He wasn't lying when he said he liked my tummy. He never shies away from stroking me there. But it brings up the Thing We Don't Talk About.

And we need to.

"Graden..."

"You insatiable wench. I need at least fifteen more minutes and maybe some food first."

I tilt my head back and look at him upside down. "Ha ha."

He leans forward and kisses my forehead. "What is it beautiful?"

"We need to talk." He freezes in a terribly stereotypical male move, so I sit up and turn to him. "Relax, will ya?"

"It's never a good thing when a woman says those words."

I shove his shoulder. "How would you know? You told me you've never been in a relationship before. But don't worry, I'm not going to ask you about feelings or anything. I think we just need to talk about the fact that we don't use protection."

His eyes darken, and I can see where his mind goes as if a movie of us is playing on his forehead. "I love feeling you raw."

"I get that. I do. I like feeling you, too. But a baby would change everything."

He gets thoughtful, like he's looking into the future. "Yeah. I'd need to rethink living on an oil rig. But maybe it's time now anyway."

Okay, this conversation is not going the way I thought it would. My face must be showing my confusion because he mirrors it back to me. I was imagining him agreeing with me. That a baby right now would be bad timing.

"It's just," I begin. "Well, we're only three days into a sexual relationship, and I don't think we're at the planning a family stage."

"I see."

Have I hurt his feelings? "For a guy who told me he's never dated, just slept with women, I'm not sure how to read your reaction, Graden."

He does that classic guy pose where he links his hands behind his head and leans back, staring at the ceiling. "We're more than 'three days into a *sexual relationship*.' I told you I love you."

"That doesn't mean you're ready to be a father to my children."

"What if I am?"

This is crazy. It doesn't make sense. "I thought it was a sex thing. You know...the whole primal biological urge. Sex talk. The risk makes it hotter, too. I didn't..."

I'm on my back before I can finish the sentence. "It's sexy as fuck to talk about breeding you, baby. To tell you I'm going to fill you with my seed. That first time, when I was pumping you full, knowing you could be getting pregnant, that was hot. After that, it was even hotter thinking you could already be pregnant. So yeah, it's partly sexual. Everything about you makes everything sexual." He grinds into me, knowing how easy I get ready for him. "But we both know it's more than that. Yeah, it's fast. Yeah, it's fucking nuts. But I love you. I want it all with you. I don't want to wait or put things off. If I learned anything from Cameron, it's that time isn't guaranteed." He grinds his hips again. "If you're not ready, we can wait. But I'm all in."

"Graden...a baby would change everything."

"So let's change everything. Let's get married."

"Married? Are you serious?"

He reaches between us, but it's not to undo his pants like I think. He's in his pocket, and he's pulling out a ring. "Serious as fuck."

The diamond is flashing in my eyes when the doorbell chimes. I start to get up, but he pushes me back down. "I'll get it. You look like you're about to pass out." He kisses me hard on my mouth and pushes off the couch.

I *am* about to pass out. I can't process anything. I'm still stuck on the idea of how hot it really is thinking I'm already pregnant—I can't even get to the part where he wants to marry me. When did he buy the ring? We went out for a bit yesterday. To the mall he says he hates. He had to be pretty sneaky, though.

He answers the door to two of our neighbor kids dressed in their uniforms selling cookies. I get up to join him as he crouches down low and talks to young Etta, who will be in my class this fall. Her mom looks like her ovaries might be exploding like fireworks at the sight of my man with her small child, and I don't blame her.

He looks good with children. Really good. And of course, Etta is wrapping him around her finger talking about camp and cookies and how she lost her tooth yesterday.

"Becks, will you bring my checkbook? It's on my dresser."

"Only if you order the peanut butter ones."

He flashes me a grin over his shoulder, and there go my ovaries. He's just amazing when he smiles.

I go into his room, a place he hasn't slept in for three days, and find there are two checkbooks on his dresser. Maybe he has a savings account or something. The first one I open says *Prime Trust Account* at the top, so I put it back and get the other, which is a personal checking account.

I get about four steps out of his room when it hits me.

Prime Trust was the name of my scholarship. Why would he have their checking account? I'm still frowning while he writes the check and brings the cookies into the kitchen.

"Where were we?" he asks. Then gets down on one knee and pulls out that ring. "Rebecca, will you marry me?"

My mind is racing a million miles an hour. The bank account. The ring. The idea that I could be carrying a baby right now. It's too much. All of it together.

I look at him and his face is earnest. He thinks he's in love. He really believes it.

But I know better.

"No."

Chapter Thirteen

GRADEN

I guess I should have been prepared. But I wasn't.

All the blood leaves my head, and I want to die. She's smart and she's right. She should hold off for someone who can give her more...you know what? Fuck that.

I will give her everything. Every damn thing.

She loves me. I know she does. And she might be smart, but she's got blinders on if she thinks this kind of love comes around more than once.

"You haven't been honest with me." She's pale and shaking, so I pull her down to the floor with me rather than chance her hurting herself if she really is going to pass out.

"What are you talking about?"

"When you sent me into your room, you forgot there were two checkbooks. One I brought to you. The other..."

Shit. "Prime Trust."

She raises her watery eyes to mine. "Well?"

"It's not what you think." I have no idea what she's thinking. It's probably exactly what she thinks.

"Tell me what it is then."

"It's not a big deal."

"Really? I think it's a pretty big deal. Either you paid for my entire college education, including room and board. Or you have somehow stolen the checkbook of a trust account and are forging checks. Something tells me it's the first one."

"I was going to tell you."

"When?" She draws her legs up like she did on the couch the other day when she was closing up on herself. "So, I'm your charity case."

"What? No."

"You paid for my education. You won't take rent for the condo." Her eyes widen. "Oh my God. The condo? You never even lived here. You got it for me, didn't you?" She slaps a palm over her forehead. "And the car. What else? Were you personally lining up all my dates for me? And when I couldn't close a deal, you stepped in and took one for the team? I'm so stupid. I thought..."

"You're not stupid. I've been taking care of you, yeah. But everything between us is real."

"Real? Are you joking right now? How can it be real if you were never honest with me? Did you get me my job too?"

I shake my head. "No, baby. I swear. That's all you. I was just trying to help. Trying to do what Cam asked. Take care of you."

She hunches over like I just hit her in the stomach. Fuck. I am bad at this. "Cameron? This is all about Cameron?" She starts rocking. "I knew it was too good to be true. You know, after he died...everything was so bad. But then things started going my way. I thought maybe he was an angel looking out for me. The scholarship, God, that was everything. I didn't have to worry about anything for four years. When I won that car...when you asked me to housesit? I should have known. The only honest thing in my life has been that no man wants to be with me. But you swooped right in to fix that, too. Didn't you?"

"It's not like that and you know it."

I put my hand on her shoulder, but she shivers away from my touch. Like I'm going to hurt her. Fuck.

"What I know, Graden, is that nothing in my life is real."

"I'm real. I swear to God, Becks. I'm real." I stop myself from reaching for her again. "You're pissed and I get that. I should have told you a long time ago about the scholarship. Cameron...he was my best friend. He loved you and your parents so much. He asked me to look out for you—and I knew I had nothing to offer but money. So I made sure you got it without ever feeling like you owed me anything. It was all for Cameron."

"You think Cameron wanted you to fuck me?"

Now I recoil like she sucker-punched me. And she did.

"No. No, I think he would make sure nobody ever found my body. I'm not good enough for you. I know that. Cam sure as hell would have known that. I never meant to fall for you."

She rolls her eyes. "Right. Because I am just impossible to resist. God. It would have been kinder for you to just tell me I was fat and plain and that's why no one wanted to go out with me twice. What you did...making me feel things that weren't true. Making me feel beautiful and wanted...that was cruel."

"Sweetheart, you are beautiful. So fucking beautiful. And I hate that I hurt you. I knew I would screw this up. Hurt you. I never meant to. When you asked me to teach you..."

"Oh, God. I am so lame." Her hands cover her face. Hiding from me.

"You are so perfect. You are everything to me." I want to touch her so bad. Wipe away all the doubts.

"Rebecca, look at me."

She shakes her head.

"C'mon, baby. Look at me."

Her hands lower. "Don't call me baby."

"I bought you a ring yesterday. Do you think I would do that just to help you get a second date with someone?"

"You have bought my entire life for five years. So, yes. It's extremely likely that you have some misplaced guilt or feelings of debt to my brother and were willing to sacrifice your future to make sure you honored your promise to him to take care of me. In fact, once you slept with me, you probably felt like you had to marry me. To appease Cam."

"You think I faked everything the last few days?"

"I don't want to. But how can I trust anything you say when you've been hiding huge secrets from me? I don't want you to feel like you have to take care of me. I want to be your equal. Your partner. Not a promise to my brother. Not a burden."

I can't believe I never thought of how she might feel finding out this way. "You're not a burden. I swear. Since the moment I stepped foot in this condo, I've been in love with you. I tried to fight it. I didn't think I was good enough for you. I still don't. And I will always take care of you. That's not going to change. Whether you're my wife or the woman who won't speak to me that I just have to fucking love from afar like some idiot from one of those romantic movies you like so much. Rebecca, you are mine, and I am yours and that will never change."

"I can't do this. I'm sorry."

"Please don't tell me this is over. I can't...please don't." It figures that the one damn time I ever wanted anything, I was going to lose it.

"I'm going to go stay with Jenn while I look for a new place to live."

Inside my head, I was screaming, but I kept a lid on it and tried to keep calm. "You don't have to do that. Stay here. I'll go. You stay."

"It's your condo. I need...I need to figure out how to build a life without my guardian angel paying all my bills. I know you were doing what you thought was best for me, and that you didn't mean to hurt me. But I'd never have let you do all this for me if I'd known. And I think you knew that or you would have been honest from the beginning. It's not just that I feel in your debt, Graden, though I do. The other problem is that you think it's in your rights to lie to me to get the desired achievement. And that's not okay. Despite your heart being in the right place, it's not okay for you to take away my choices or protect me from the truth." She paused. "You need to let me go."

"I don't think I can do that."

"You need to figure out how. And I need to learn how to stand on my own, without your help."

She's already made up her mind. The shell-shocked gaze is gone, and in its place, a quiet determined look. "Will you give me a chance? Please, Rebecca."

"I don't ever see us being together. Not really."

My heart cracks like she's wielding a sledgehammer instead of a steely reserve. "And what if you're pregnant?"

"I'll call you. I promise."

Because she is honest and wouldn't hide things from me. Unlike me.

I know I need to let her go. I won't give up. But I understand what she's saying. She's independent, and I have been keeping her in a cage without even telling her.

I honestly don't know how to go back to the guy I was even a month ago.

I guess I taught her how to break me after all.

Chapter Fourteen

REBECCA

Two Months Later

I switch the phone to my other ear and Jenn is still chattering. "Come out with us," she says.

I look down at my outfit.

Not a chance.

"I'm tired."

"You're always tired."

"Those kids wear me out. You hang out with five-year-olds all day and then tell me you want to go hang out in a bar with men who are more immature than the kids were."

I have a busy night planned. Wine. Pizza. Chocolate. Bridget Jones.

Jenn sighs. "None of the men are ever going to compare to Graden for you. You should just call him."

I look around my tiny apartment. It's a studio on top of someone's garage, but it's within walking distance of the school. Which is good because I sold my car to start paying Graden back. "I can't call him." He's probably back on the rig anyway.

I wonder what he's going to do with the condo now. Will he rent it out? Will he even keep it? It's not my business, and I shouldn't care.

But I do and I always will.

My apartment is just right for me now, though. I got what little furniture I have from thrift stores, painting it all white. The walls are soothing mint, and I put lace on everything and anything. It's all feminine and all mine. The condo, which is really nice, was very masculine and sparsely decorated. I never felt like I could do what I wanted with it since I was "housesitting."

So, I vomited girliness all over my new place.

"Go have fun, Jenn. I'm really fine here. I don't want to go out, and I'm not secretly hoping you'll cajole me into changing my mind."

"Okay. But what if I cajole you into calling Graden?"

I crumple a piece of paper near the mic on my phone. "What's that? Are you going through a tunnel? You're breaking up."

"Ha ha. Fine. But brunch tomorrow."

"Absolutely. Have fun."

It occurs to me, while watching Renee Zellweger singing alone in her apartment, that I am...becoming pathetic. I've given up on going out there. I don't want to try anymore. I'm only twenty-three. I have one three-day relationship and a string of bad first dates under my belt. It's too soon to give up. But the thought of anyone else touching me. No. Just no.

The thought of Graden touching me. Well, that's better.

What would I do if he knocked on my door? I pause the movie and lean back, closing my eyes. I undo the belt of my robe. I am, pathetically, wearing the nightie from the shopping mall beneath it. It was staring at me from the drawer, wondering why I never wear it, and I figured, what the hell?

It's a good thing I don't have a spare wedding dress hanging in the closet or I'd probably sit around the house in it, too.

I take a deep breath and bring my hand up to the little black panties. I imagine Graden and...I hear a knock at the door?

Fucking Jenn. She ruined a perfectly good orgasm and is wasting both our time. I do not want to go out tonight.

I swing the door open. "Go away!"

"Uh, bad time?"

I imagine my eyes are cartoonishly round as I stare at Graden. Graden!

"Wh-what are you doing here?"

He starts to answer then stops, taking in my appearance. Shit. I forgot to belt my robe.

He swallows hard. "I've interrupted." His brow furrows into wrinkles of pain. "I'm sorry. Here's your mail." He thrusts two envelopes into my hand and turns to go.

I think about letting him leave believing there is another man here. That I'm wearing the nightie from that day for someone else. It would be infinitely less embarrassing than the truth: that I'm wearing it all by myself because I'm a lonely spinster. But I call out, "Graden, wait."

He stops at the bottom of the stairs and looks up. God, the stricken expression on his face guts me. I belt the robe. "Please come up. You're not interrupting anything. There's nobody here."

Eyebrows raised, he stalks back up the stairs slowly. God, he looks amazing. This is the first time I've seen him since I moved out. He's better than the mental pictures my memory served up.

A hot flush steals over me as he gets closer. All that towering strength. All those corded, bunching muscles. I swallow hard and try to still my heart. It's thumping so hard he can probably see it.

And I'm wet.

He stops in front of me on the landing. "You smell good, sugar."

I hold it together for another second or two while we stare into each other's eyes. And then I start to cry.

Big, stupid, gushing tears. And I crumple into him.

"Oh, baby, don't cry." He sweeps me into his embrace and brings me into the house.

"I don't even know why I'm crying," I protest, but I nestle my face into his neck. He doesn't smell like cookies, but oh my God, does he smell amazing. He doesn't wear cologne—it's the scent of his soap and shampoo and just him. Just him.

He settles us onto the little couch and soothes me, rubbing small circles on my back. "I didn't mean to make you cry."

I pull back to look at him. "It's not your fault. It's just that...I miss you."

"I miss you, too. God, Becks. More than you know." He cups my cheek. "I've been going crazy."

"Me, too."

Graden kisses my forehead. I can feel his arousal beneath me. He's hard and ready to take me. All that's standing between us is my stupid pride.

I swallow hard. Swallow the ball of pride that's made me miserable for two months. Yes, I can do it. I can take care of myself. I can pay my bills and get along day to day. But it's half a life. It's certainly not the life I want.

I undo the belt one last time and shrug out of the robe. His eyes dilate as he takes me in.

"I wore this tonight so I could think of you while I touched myself and dreamed about what could have been."

His hand squeezes my leg and a guttural groan escapes him. "Becks."

"I don't want to dream about you anymore."

Chapter Fifteen

GRADEN

I'm on the edge of a cliff and I'm afraid to breathe.

She's here. She with me. I'm finally touching my woman again, and for the first time in my life, I am fucking scared.

She shifts, and I'm afraid she's going to get up and kick me out. Instead, she straddles me, that moist heat right where I need it most. "You have to be honest with me. From now on. If I can ever learn to trust in you...in myself...again...you can't keep things from me."

Something that feels like sunshine lights up inside my chest. Is she going to give me another chance? "Baby, whatever you want. I promise."

"I don't ever want to feel like that again. I don't want to wonder if you're just acting or doing something because you think it's the honorable thing to do. I want you to want me. Just me."

I open my palm, and she gasps. "Put this fucking ring on and you will never, ever doubt me again. I promise."

She lets out a watery laugh. "That's a pretty romantic proposal."

"You never said you wanted romance."

"You've been holding that since you got here?"

I nod. God. If this doesn't work. I don't think I can go back to a world without her in it. "I know I don't deserve you. If Cam were here..."

"If Cam were here, he would kick your ass. And then he would give you a beer and tell you all the ways you aren't allowed to screw up with me. And then he would give you his blessing because he loved you, Graden. Just like I love you."

"I'm not on the rig anymore. They transferred me to an office job. I kept the condo, but if you'd rather live in a house or a treehouse or a cave, you just tell me and we'll move." I look around. "Maybe not here though."

She laughs. "You do look a little ridiculous with all this lace."

"Put on the fucking ring." I clear my throat. "Please."

"You can be a little domineering, you know."

"A little?" I take her hand and put the ring on it myself. It looks real good. I feel like I can breathe again when she doesn't tear it off. "You like it when I'm domineering." I'm going to remember this moment for the rest of my life. "You like it when I tell you what to do."

"In bed, yes. Try it anywhere else, I dare you."

Adrenaline rushes through me like I've just walked away from an explosion and my hands start to shake. "I came so close to losing you. I don't think I'm man enough to go through that ever again."

I squeeze her hard. Probably too hard. Her curves fit into my hands like they were made to be there. She arches into my hold on her. My goddess. Mine.

"We don't have to go fast. If you want to wait for the wedding. For the babies. I get it. I rushed us last time. I brought condoms. Just in case. I mean, I don't expect you to have sex with me tonight. We can. I just don't want you to think I expect it."

Jesus. I sound like a real idiot.

"I don't want to go slow." She rolls her hips over my erection. "I feel like my life has been on hold until right now. I want it all. I'm ready if you are."

"I changed my mind about going slow. Babe, I need to fuck you." I won't feel right again until I do. Until I'm deep inside her. I can't think straight now. I squeeze her plump ass and groan. "Right now."

She's undoing my jeans and we maneuver enough to get them down to my ankles without unseating that hot pussy. She grinds on me, the friction of the silky panties feels good. But not as good as the vise of her cunt is going to feel.

I grasp one string on her hip and yank, tearing the fabric to her astounded gasp. "I'll buy you new ones."

And then she's sliding up and down my length and I'm lost in her eyes. I know we are both trying to prolong this, but I need inside her. I still her and notch myself at the gates of heaven. "You sure you don't want a condom?"

Please say...

"No condom."

Thank God.

Rebecca slides down my pole slowly, and we both groan. She is so wet and juicy. When she's seated all the way, when my balls are touching her ass, she starts undulating those womanly hips in slow circles. I look down at where we are joined, her sweet lips stretched tight around my girth, and I bite my lip to keep myself from ramming hard. The air is sawing in and out of me like I want my cock in her to be doing.

Nothing has ever felt like this before. Not even our first time. Because there are no secrets between us now. I'm not behind the scenes controlling her life. She chose me. She can survive without me, but she doesn't want to.

She pulls the hem of my shirt up, so I help her get it off me. She leans over and flicks one of my nipples with her tongue, and my hips arch off the couch. "Becks," I warn.

Then she bites it.

"Fuck," I roar, digging my fingers into her hips, I let go of my restraint.

I'm fucking her hard and she's taking it, making this sweet keening sound I feel in my bones. She tilts her head back and holds on to me like she's riding a bull.

And then she surrenders.

She's pulling me deeper inside, milking me. The feminine rhythm is so beautiful and wild. I can't stop myself from joining her, filling her up with the essence of who I am and what I was made to do. Fuck, if we aren't making a baby right now. And the thought brings another pulse from my dick.

She's mine. I smooth my thumb down the column of her throat and feel her erratic pulse there. Her eyes fly open and a secret smile graces her pretty face.

"I love you, Rebecca. I swear you'll never doubt that another day of your life. I know I suck at relationship stuff. But I'll spend the rest of my life trying to get better."

"I love you, Graden. And I don't think you suck as bad as you think you do."

She rolls her hips and I start to harden again. "You think I can get through this whole night without pulling out of you once?"

She reaches back and unties her sweet nightie, pulling it off and showing me that body that's haunted my dreams since she walked away. I latch on to one breast and quit talking for a while.

Epilogue

REBECCA,

Two Years Later

I'm standing in front of the window of the lingerie shop and it's now or never.

Beetlejuice, better known as Bethany, our fifteen-month-old, is snoozing in her stroller. I could never bring her in there when she's awake. She's an escape artist, and it's because of her that I can't have nice things.

Except that she's the best, nicest thing that ever happened to her daddy and me.

I push the stroller into the store and try to take in everything at once. I don't know how long my window of opportunity is before the little monster wakes up, so I need to shop fast if I want to surprise Graden.

A slender woman approaches and then we both smile when we recognize each other. Leslie. She gives me a hug and tells me my baby looks sweet.

"All babies look sweet when they're asleep," I tell her.

"Are you okay? You look a little..." She's searching for a word that means tired and worn-out, but one that wouldn't offend me.

"I'm exhausted. You can say it."

Leslie tsked. "Seems like Graden is the kind of guy who would help you out more."

"How do you know I ended up with Graden?" I ask.

She picks up my left hand. "I helped him pick out this ring to surprise you."

What? "The day we were here together?"

She nods. "Yeah, he called me. Asked me to pick out five rings and I sent him pictures from my phone. My friend at the jeweler across the way held them, and two days later he ran down here while you were in the bathroom to buy it."

"Wow. I had no idea. I remember wondering how he'd managed to get it." My heart bloomed and my face heated.

"Still a blushing bride, I see."

"He takes good care of me still. Of us. It's not his fault I'm tired." I pause. "Actually, it is his fault. I'm telling him tonight that I'm pregnant again. I was hoping to wear something with no spit-up on it. And maybe a little forgiving of some of my newer curves."

Leslie hugs me again and helps me pick out the perfect nightgown. We exchange numbers so I can invite her to the baby shower, and when Bethany wakes up, we're already halfway to the car.

I just hope that Graden is okay with this. We haven't talked about having another baby—this one is more than a handful and runs us both ragged. I know he'll love another child—but will he be excited about one?

GRADEN

I TAKE A QUICK, HOT shower after finally getting the baby to sleep. I don't know how my wife handles her alone all day long. She says she wants to be a stay-at-home mom for now, but man, Bethany has to be more work than a classroom full of kindergarteners.

I come out of the bathroom to find my wife dressed in a hot little turquoise nightie that gets me instantly hard. Until I see she's passed out.

I get her tucked in, removing all the decorative pillows she insists we need on the bed every day, when I see what looks like a flat pen tucked under one.

Holy shit. It's a pregnancy test.

I'm sure she meant to present it to me while...conscious. But I can't wait until morning, so I look.

It's positive.

Holy shit.

Is she happy? Excited? Resigned? I don't want to wake her up since she obviously needs all the sleep she can get.

Am I happy?

Her last pregnancy crosses my mind. The way she waddled. Her cravings. The feel of the baby kicking my hand. Holding Bethany for the first time.

Yeah. Yeah, I'm fucking stoked.

I can't believe I'm the same guy who didn't want a family. Or a wife. Or even a home. My girls are everything to me now. Life is crazy most of the time. But it's good crazy. It's damn good crazy.

My childhood was a mess—but that just means I try harder. Give my kid the stability I never had. Give my wife the love my mom was always looking for but was too drugged out to ever find.

I spoon around my wife and put my hand on her belly where our baby grows.

"I'll keep my promise, Cameron," I whisper, in case he's listening. "I'll take care of your baby sister until my last breath."

HAPPY SIGH...DON'T you just love happy endings?

Did you enjoy Graden and Rebecca? That combination of sweet and filthy? There's more where that came from. **The Blue Collar Bad Boys** series is just beginning. Sexy bad boys who do sexy bad things with their rough hands and the innocent virgins who love them. What's not to like?

Don't miss the burly tow truck driver and the sassy, uptown sorority girl in the next book Wrecked[1].

IF YOU'RE TIRED OF billionaires, maybe you're ready for some real men. Dirty, hardworking, and good with their hands are the kind of heroes you'll find in the *Blue Collar Bad Boy Series*. These guys aren't cultured. They are hot *AF* alpha heroes who know how to take care of the slightly nerdy women they fall for. For reals, this series is more fun than you knew you were missing. And they don't need to be read in order.

So which blue collar bad boy will you choose next? They are all rough, raw, and surprisingly sweet.

Like...the roadhouse bouncer and the actuarial sciences student in *Bounced*[2].

Or...the carpenter and the Jeopardy! nerd in *Nailed*[3].

Perhaps...the oil rigger and the kindergarten teacher in *Drilled*[4].

Mayhap...the tow truck driver and the sorority uptown girl in *Wrecked*[5].

Surely...the brick layer hot single dad and the babysitter in *Laid*[6].

---

1.   https://books2read.com/u/bzaBZE

2.   *https://books2read.com/Bounced*

3.   *https://books2read.com/Nailed*

4.   *https://books2read.com/Drilled*

5.   *https://books2read.com/wrecked*

6.   *https://books2read.com/laid*

How about...a returning military hero and the wallflower at Christmas in *Tagged*[7]?

Or...the farmer who needs a wife and wants the curvy waitress in *Plowed*[8]?

Or...the hot rancher trying to convince the city girl to stay in *Bucked*[9]?

Maybe...the bomb squad cop and his pregnant neighbor? Did I mention she's a virgin? You read that right. Try *Banged*[10].

And surely...the modern day Viking bartender and the bookworm virgin in *Tapped*[11]?

About the author

LIKE FIRST TIMES? FORBIDDEN fruit? *Yes, please.*

Love a hot, dominant alpha claiming what's his? *Fuck, yeah.*

Want to watch him fall hard for the sweetest fantasy he didn't know he needed? Me too!

I'm Brill Harper and I love happily ever afters, smokin' hot bad boys, and quirky, often nerdy, heroines that I'd love to be friends with off page. These ladies are not perfect—but they're perfect for one man—and he's always sexy AF.

Seriously—these heroes only have one weakness, and it's sticky, sweet love. They don't let anything stand in the way of taking what belongs to them. When it comes to the women they love, it's hard cocks, dirty talk, and soft, mushy heart feels.

---

7.   https://books2read.com/tagged

8.   https://books2read.com/plowed

9.   https://books2read.com/bucked

10.   https://books2read.com/banged

11.   https://books2read.com/Tapped-A-Blue-Collar-Bad-Boy-Book

*Brill is a sooper sekrit penname for a better known author who just can't handle all the dirty. She can't handle it...but can you?

BookBub[12]

---

12.   https://www.bookbub.com/authors/brill-harper

Also by Brill Harper

Blue Collar Bad Boys
Bounced: A Blue Collar Bad Boys Book
Nailed: A Blue Collar Bad Boys Book
Drilled: A Blue Collar Bad Boys Book
Wrecked: A Blue Collar Bad Boys Book
Laid: A Blue Collar Bad Boys Book
Tagged: A Blue Collar Bad Boys Christmas
Plowed: A Blue Collar Bad Boys Book
Bucked: A Blue Collar Bad Boys Book
Banged: A Blue Collar Bad Boys Book
Tapped: A Blue Collar Bad Boy Book

It's Complicated
All Together
All at Once

Love in Brazen Bay
Wrong Number Text
The Right Stuff
So Wrong It's Right

Don't Get Me Wrong

Standalone
Dirty Jobs: a Blue Collar Bad Boys Collection
Notch on His Bedpost
Honeymoon With The Prince::A Modern Day Fairy Tale
Good Girl

Watch for more at https://brillharper.com.